"You Could Always Arrange to Have a Male Escort to Parties, Pilar . . ."

Trace said gruffly. "I don't believe that you haven't had volunteers."

Something about the way he looked at her set off little twinges of unease.

"In case you haven't noticed," she replied, "there isn't exactly a surfeit of single males over the age of thirty in Natchez. Besides, I'm not that desperate for a man."

"Aren't you?"

"No, I'm not," she retorted.

"You want to be looked at, but you don't want to be touched . . . by anyone. Is that it?" he murmured.

Pilar avoided his eyes. "I don't know what you're talking about."

"I'm not sure that I do, either," he said dryly.

Books by Janet Dailey

The Glory Game
The Pride of Hannah Wade
Silver Wings, Santiago Blue
Calder Born, Calder Bred
Stands a Calder Man
This Calder Range
This Calder Sky
The Best Way To Lose
For the Love of God
Foxfire Light
The Hostage Bride
The Lancaster Men
Mistletoe & Holly
The Second Time
Separate Cabins
Terms of Surrender
Western Man
Night Way
Ride the Thunder
The Rogue
Touch the Wind

Published by POCKET BOOKS

Most Pocket Books are available at special quantity discounts for bulk purchases for sales promotions, premiums or fund raising. Special books or book excerpts can also be created to fit specific needs.

For details write the office of the Vice President of Special Markets, Pocket Books, 1230 Avenue of the Americas, New York, New York 10020.

Janet Dailey
The Best Way To Lose

PUBLISHED BY POCKET BOOKS NEW YORK

POCKET BOOKS, a division of Simon & Schuster, Inc.
1230 Avenue of the Americas, New York, N.Y. 10020

Originally published by Silhouette Books.

ISBN: 0-671-62510-1

First Pocket Books printing August, 1986

10 9 8 7 6 5 4 3 2 1

Map by Ray Lundgren

POCKET and colophon are registered trademarks of Simon & Schuster, Inc.

Printed in the U.S.A.

The Best Way To Lose

Chapter One

Dr. Webster. Dr. Webster, please report to Emergency. Dr. Webster." Striking chimes preceded the call by the disembodied voice paging through the hospital corridors.

The sounds, the smells permeating the air, all seemed intensified to Pilar Santee as she stood by the window in the waiting room. Her slim body was tense almost to the point of rigidity. Everything seemed so loud—the hushed murmur of worried voices within the room, the rustle of polyester uniforms in the hallways, the alerting chimes of the hospital page. Like the strong, medicinally antiseptic odor that burned her nose, they had a highly irritating quality.

"Would you like some coffee, Pilar?" The

soft, solicitous inquiry came from a point near her elbow.

Stiffly Pilar turned from the window and checked the impulse to respond with a sharp negative. The rawness of her violently churning emotions and aggravated senses had darkened her eyes to near-black. For an instant Pilar could only stare at the lingering traces of shock and tears in Sandra Kay's face. The sight of all that sympathy from her friend nearly sickened her.

"No, thank you." It was a taut and quick reply.

Her glance swung to the others who had gathered in the waiting room to share this vigil with her. All their expressions showed some form of deep concern. It seemed such a contradiction to her own feelings, which were dominated by anger. Her agitation increased because it was so wrong to feel this way. Pilar glanced at the heirloom ring on her wedding finger and rubbed it absently as if it were some kind of talisman. She didn't understand why her eyes were so dry. Why wasn't she upset like the others? Elliot was her husband.

It became imperative to get out, to get away from all this caring sympathy. She didn't understand the raw, raging anger that was bottled inside, and she was much too well bred to let it show.

"Excuse me," she murmured tautly as she started to walk by Sandra Kay Austin. "I'm going to step out for a moment."

"I'll come with you."

"No." Pilar paused, fighting the hot urges to scream at her friend that she wanted to be alone. With brittle control she managed to insist, "I'd rather you would stay here with the others. I won't be long."

There was hesitation in Sandra Kay's expression, an unwillingness to accept that Pilar really meant what she said. Before the searching gaze could uncover the feelings Pilar was trying to contain, she walked to the door and into the hallway. Her steps immediately slowed, her glance drawn to the closed door of the Intensive Care Unit room. She'd been allowed to see him once—for a very few minutes only.

Her unusually acute hearing caught part of a remark made by someone in the waiting room. "—taking it very well." She wanted to laugh, because she was "taking it" badly. Snatches of other conversations came rushing back. "—collapsed on the tennis court— massive coronary—heart damage—" Rage tumbled inside her, driving her forward.

The chapel sign beckoned to her. With a challenging tilt of her dark head, Pilar entered the hallowed sanctuary. Beneath all the taut anger, there was a desperate wish that, here, she would find relief from these bitterly resentful feelings.

A deep stillness surrounded her as she moved quietly to the polished oak pew in the front and sat down. Her gaze became fixed on the cross at the altar. The strength of her faith had always been something she could rely on, but it seemed to have forsaken her.

Pilar sat very still and very quiet, her hands folded calmly in the lap of her smoke-blue skirt and her head unbowed. Light spilled from the altar to shine on her proud features and sable-black hair. Her mind's eye brought back the riling image of Elliot as she had last seen him—so deathly pale, tubes stuck in his arms and nose, with all sorts of monitoring gadgets attached to him and surrounded by beeping machines.

A raw groan came from her throat, almost animal in its origin. It wasn't fair that this should happen to Elliot . . . with no warning . . . no reason. He was in excellent physical shape, trimly muscled and lean. Someone, attempting to comfort her, had tried to assure her that sudden attacks were to be expected for a man of Elliot's age. Pilar violently rejected that reasoning. Elliot Santee was unquestionably the youngest fifty-five-year-old man she'd ever met.

Anger trembled again, an emotion that should have been alien in this place of worship. Pilar quietly sank to her knees in front of the altar, clasping her hands in a prayerful pose and resting them on the smooth railing. But no words of prayer came to her lips.

All she could remember was the way she constantly teased Elliot about his daily ritual of exercise—jogging, swimming, and weight lifting, plus a couple of games of golf or tennis each week. And Elliot, so handsome and charismatic, had always teased her back, insisting that a man his age had to stay in shape when he had such a young bride. After five years of marriage he still referred to her as his bride, surprising her with gifts of flowers or jewelry for no reason at all other than a desire to give.

Their May-December marriage had raised many an eyebrow in Natchez and brought forecasts of its early demise, but their age difference had never bothered them. It was something they joked about. Elliot was always fond of bragging that he'd swept Pilar off her twenty-four-year-old feet when they'd first met.

So many plans for the future had been made, so many things they wanted to do together. It wasn't right that he might be taken from her. Pilar railed against the thought, violently opposing the very idea of it.

A hand touched her shoulder and she cast a startled glance upward into the benignly sympathetic eyes of the minister from their church. He smiled gently.

"I thought I might find you here, Mrs. Santee." When she started to stand up, his hand increased its pressure slightly to prevent the movement. "Let me join you in prayer."

As he knelt at the railing beside her, Pilar was plagued by the hypocrisy of her emotions. She didn't want to pray; she wanted to demand. She wasn't righteous—she was indignant.

"Our heavenly Father . . ." As the minister

began Pilar shut her eyes and ears to the words she couldn't genuinely support. His quiet voice droned in the background of her hearing while she remembered how Elliot had carried her up the stairs of their beautiful antebellum home in Natchez just last week. Which was hardly the sort of thing to be recalling at this particular moment. ". . . and give comfort to those who love him. Amen."

Unclasping her clenched fingers, Pilar pushed at the railing to lever herself upright the instant he finished. "Thank you, Reverend Chasmore." Her finely controlled expression showed none of the emotions smoldering within.

He was slower to rise. "It was my pleasure, Mrs. Santee." Again he spoke in a comforting tone. "I hope you haven't tried to reach me earlier. I was out calling on some of my parishioners and decided to stop by to make my hospital rounds before returning to the parsonage. Mrs. Parker in Admissions told me the news about your husband."

"Yes." She searched for something to say. "It was very good of you to come." Words without meaning, polite phrases spoken because they were expected.

"Have you taken the time to eat something since you've been here?" The minister fell in step with her as she turned away from the altar and walked to the door. Her soul had supposedly been nourished by prayer, so now he was trying to see that her body was fed.

"No. I'm really not hungry," she replied

firmly even though she had missed the late breakfast Cassie had been preparing for her when Field Carlton had come by to break the news to her.

"Mrs. Austin told me you haven't left the waiting room since you arrived this morning." It was a benevolent reproach. "Why don't you come to the cafeteria with me and have some coffee?"

"Honestly, I don't want anything," Pilar insisted, struggling not to snap at him. She sensed his desire to press the issue, but the set of her features seemed to make him hesitate as he opened the chapel door for her to exit the quiet room.

"I'm not certain if you were informed that the authorities were successful in contacting your husband's son. I understand he's on his way to Natchez now."

"Good." Her response was short and completely indifferent to the information. In her five years of marriage to Elliot she had seen his son no more than three times. There was no estrangement between father and son; they had simply never been close even though Trace Santee worked in the family-owned barge line. Pilar had long ago stopped trying to reason out why it was so. Neither Elliot nor his son had appeared to be bothered by the infrequent communication between themselves, so Pilar had ceased to be concerned by it.

"Are you certain you won't reconsider my invitation and come to the cafeteria? We can leave word at the nurse's station where you'll be if there's any change in your husband's condition," the minister assured her. "You really should have something, if only a cup of soup."

"No, thank you. Cassie will fix me something when I go home tonight." *If* she went home—but Pilar didn't raise that point.

The same group of close family friends were in the waiting room when she returned to it, even though only members of the immediate family were permitted to see Elliot, and only for specified periods. As Sandra Kay had said, they wanted to sit with her during the long vigil. Pilar knew she should have been moved by their thoughtfulness, but she truly wanted to be alone. She also knew they would never understand if she told them that, so she silently rejoined them to await further word from the doctor on his prognosis.

The props of the tender's motor boiled coffee-colored foam in the stern's wake as the boat bucked the current of the silt-laden waters of the Mississippi River and aimed for the landing below a high bluff. Old wooden buildings were tucked back against the wall of the bluff—all that remained of the notorious hellhole of a town along the waterfront area known as Natchez-under-the-Hill. The long rays of a late-afternoon sun struck the buildings full force, glaringly revealing their age. There was a lot of talk about rebuilding the area as a tourist attraction, but it was mostly talk with some refurbishing accompanying it.

Nothing changed, it seemed. Trace carried the half-smoked cigarette to his mouth, protectively cupping his hand around it to keep the wind from blowing any hot ash from the tip—a holdover from the times he'd pushed oil barges up the river. A worn captain's hat was pulled low on his forehead, slightly off center in a rakish touch. His strong, jutting features were leather-tan from hours spent outdoors, and sun lines sprayed from the corners of his steel-gray eyes, their color made to appear an even lighter shade by ink-black lashes that matched the thick eyebrows and shaggy hair.

As the tender from the towboat approached the landing, Trace tossed the cigarette over the side and reached for the duffel bag at his feet. There was a suggestion of impatience in the rippling muscles under the faded denim jacket. The small boat maneuvered close to the bank and Trace stood up, easily balancing on his river legs, and heaved his duffel bag ashore. He threw a glance at the man at the tiller.

"Tell Ned I'll buy him dinner the next time we meet up," he said, raising his voice to make himself heard above the noise of the idling motor holding the boat in position by the bank.

With an agile leap, he was ashore and hefting his duffel bag onto his shoulder. Trace paused to toss a saluting wave in the direction of the towboat, its engines screaming while it pushed a dozen fully loaded barges lashed together up the channel of the mighty river. A horn tooted in reply, and the hard mouth almost quirked into a smile, then sobered as Trace turned to face the long, steep hill to the town at the top of the bluff.

Shifting the bag more squarely onto his shoulder, he started up the hill, long easy strides carrying him smoothly along. His frayed denims rode comfortably on his narrow hips, the frequency of wearing shaping them to his leanly muscled thighs and legs. Despite the steep climb Trace was barely out of breath when he reached the top of the hill, where the town of Natchez spread out before him.

The last time he was back, two years ago, it had been a two-taxi town. It seemed unlikely that the cab company had expanded. He stepped into the street and followed the curb line, sticking out his thumb to the first vehicle that passed by. It didn't stop and Trace kept walking. Another car came and went, weaving out around him.

There was a short burst of a police siren as he turned around to face the front again. The police car was in the oncoming lane of the narrow street. The patrolman stuck his head out the window.

"Hitchhiking is against the law—" Recognition broke across the older man's expression. "Santee? Trace Santee? Is that you?" He pulled the patrol car into the opposite curb while Trace waited for a car to pass before crossing the street.

"Hey, Digger. How's it going?" he laconically greeted the graying man who had been a fixture on the local police force for as many years as Trace could remember.

The officer shoved a pudgy hand out the window to shake hands with him. "Trace Santee, you ol' rakehell son of a gun, how the hell are you?!" Digger Jones declared with a wide grin. "That's a new scar on your cheek, isn't it? No need to ask whether you've had any better luck staying out of trouble. Ya gotta learn to stay out of those riverfront dives."

Trace absently rubbed the faint white scar that slashed his cheek and smiled indifferently. "Some Cajun got a little free with his knife one night."

"It couldn't be that you were messin' around with his gal?" the officer chided with a knowing look.

There was a faint lift of one shoulder. "She wasn't objecting." He leaned a hand on the hood of the patrol car, bracing himself easily with it. "I need a ride to the hospital. How about giving me a lift?"

"Yeah, I guess you heard about your daddy." A grim kind of sympathy flashed across the aging lines of the man's face, shortly replaced by a half-hearted smile. "I'll take you there. An' for a change, you can ride in the front seat."

Trace circled around the car to the passenger side, stowed his bag in the back seat, then climbed in the front. As Trace shut the door Digger shifted into driving gear and swung the car back into the street, making an illegal U-turn.

"You're an emergency." Digger Jones briefly slid a smile at him. "I wondered how long it would take them to track you down."

"I wasn't hard to find." Trace settled loosely into the seat, showing a relaxed composure, but his fingers were lightly drumming on the door's armrest—restless, impatient energy always just below the surface. "I took the *Betty Lou* out this time. I got the radio call when we were halfway between here and nowhere, headed downstream. Ned Hanks happened by, and it was quicker to catch a ride with him than wait until we reached a town." He leveled a glance at the officer with disconcerting directness. "How's Elliot?"

Trace Santee had been rowdy as a youngster, giving Digger all kinds of trouble. There had been times when some had given up on him, calling him wild and worthless, but Digger never had. Maybe because he liked the way Trace looked a man square in the eyes.

"Ten years on the river sure hasn't tamed you down any." Digger absently prefaced his reply with an observation. "It looks real bad, Trace."

"I figured that." There was a slow swing of his gaze to the road ahead of the patrol car. "But you're wrong about the river. It's taught me some things. I roll with the flow now instead of fighting it every inch of the way. I discovered I don't get caught in quite so many eddies and undercurrents that way." The corners of his mouth lifted in a lazy movement as he slid a sleepy glance at the driver.

"Glad to hear it." Digger nodded in an approving fashion. "Wisdom doesn't come with age. If you don't have it now, you never will. You must be—what—" He measured Trace with a quick glance, trying to put the years together. "Thirty-four? Thirty-five?"

"Thirty-five."

"It's about time you got smart," Digger stated. "Being a wild fool when you're young—well, that's to be expected. But when you're older, hell, you're just an old fool."

"Like my father?" It was softly suggested, a hint of challenge in its very quietness. But Trace was looking out the windshield when Digger glanced in his direction, and he spoke again before Digger had to come up with an adequate response or ignore the comment. "I heard Elliot was playing tennis when he had the attack. I suppose his wife was with him." There was a slight narrowing of his gaze as he looked at some distant point down the road.

"No. I talked to Cassie. It seems Elliot had jogged over to Booth Carlton's place for a game of tennis early this morning. Mrs. Santee was just sitting down to breakfast when Booth's youngest son, Field, came over to fetch her. They arrived at the hospital about the same time the ambulance got there with Elliot." The officer shook his head with wondering confusion. "Always exercising, your daddy was. Always pushing himself to keep that young-looking body of his. He pushed himself too hard this time."

"He always had to compete—and he always had to win." The recollection tugged the corners of Trace's mouth downward with a faint grimness.

It seemed his relationship with Elliot Santee had always been one of rivalry—competing with each other for his mother's affections when she was alive, then shifting to other fields until Trace had dropped out of the game somewhere around the age of fifteen. For a long while he had believed he'd outgrown that competitive urge—until the last few years, when it had welled strong within him again.

"Maybe I shouldn't say it . . ." Digger paused to draw in a deep breath. ". . . but your daddy never played any game unless he was damned sure he could win it before it started. He never did like bucking the odds. And the odds aren't too good for him this time."

Before Trace entered the private waiting room off the Intensive Care Unit, he met the doctor attending his father and cornered him to obtain the full particulars. He pressed for substantiated answers until he got them, indifferent to the doctor's irritation at his persistence.

When he entered the waiting room, he was

met by the auburn-haired Sandra Kay Austin, only a few years older than himself. Glancing at the handful of people in the room, he noticed that most of them were somewhere around their forties. As his father grew older his circle of close friends had grown younger.

"Trace, I'm so glad you're here." Sandra Kay clutched at his arm when he slung his duffel bag into an out-of-the-way corner. The level of her voice dropped to a conspiratorial pitch. "Paul and I can't stay any longer. We sent the boys over to his mother's, but they're going out tonight and we simply have to get home. But I just didn't want to leave Pilar here alone. She needs someone with her at a time like this. You'll look after her, won't you?"

"Yes, I will." He nodded stiffly.

"I knew you wouldn't be a rat about this," she declared with a relieved smile, indifferent to the backhanded insult she'd just delivered by implying that he was capable of uncouthness. "Try to convince her to eat something. She hasn't had anything all day. She's barely been out of this room except once to see Elliot and pray in the chapel. She's putting on a brave front, but I know she's scared sick like the rest of us."

"We're all very worried about him," Trace agreed and finally let his gaze stray to the window where his father's wife stood. Yellow sunlight poured through the window, showering the tall, ebony-haired woman with its golden hues.

"Paul and I will let Pilar know we're leaving."

Either his arrival or the Austins' departure seemed to signal the exodus of the rest. Trace stood to one side and observed the comforting hugs and warm kisses each bestowed on his father's wife, along with encouraging words of hope.

The room became oddly silent when only the two of them remained to occupy it. Trace removed his much-worn captain's hat and combed his fingers through his black hair, rumpling the flatness left by the hat. Then he held the cap in both hands to keep them busy so they wouldn't get other ideas about holding something else.

"Hello, Pilar." It was a bland greeting, too contained and too reserved.

Pilar held the directness of those gray eyes for a few seconds while he wandered leisurely across the room to the window. A sudden resentment flared at the sight of such healthy male vigor, so strong and rugged. The sweaty male smell of him merely seemed to emphasize his virility. It made no sense, but she hated him for standing there when his father was lying in a hospital bed, stuck full of tubes and wires and needles. That anger was back, impotent and frustrating.

"Hello, Trace." Always she searched for some resemblance to Elliot and found none. Elliot was handsome and urbane while there was something earthy about his son.

She walked past him, twisting her fingers together in distressed agitation. With her friends she'd had little desire for conversation. She had even less with Trace Santee, who was virtually a stranger to her. But he was Elliot's son. Out of consideration for him, she felt a sense of duty to go through the motions.

"I don't know how much you were told about what happened and the extent of . . ." Pilar faltered, her poise breaking for the first time at the task of verbally expressing the very situation she so violently resented.

"There's no need to fill me in on the details," Trace inserted into the involuntary pause.

He could hear the strain in her voice. When she turned to face him again, he observed the tension around her mouth and eyes. He also noticed the absence of swollen, puffy eyelids and the redness from tears. Whatever she was feeling, it was locked up inside. There was a slow traveling of his gaze over her face to take in its smoldering beauty, the classic cheekbones and warm red lips.

There was so much fire there, so much passion. Trace swung away before wayward urges took hold of him. The first time he'd met her, it had been at the wedding. At the time he'd joked that he was sure she'd understand if he didn't call her "Mother." Only it hadn't been a joke. With each passing year the humor had faded until it was no longer something to laugh about. Nagged by guilt over the feelings the sight of his father's wife aroused in him, Trace had kept his distance and channeled all that restless energy into other pursuits.

A vinyl-covered chair was in front of him and Trace lowered himself into it, stretching out his long legs and hooking his hat over the end of the armrest. It wasn't easy to keep his eyes off her. His glance traveled up the shapely calf of her leg to the hem of the smoky blue skirt, then made a quick run to her face.

"I thought you'd want to know what happened." There was something half angry about the curtness of her statement that seemed to challenge him for his lack of concern.

"Digger Jones gave me a ride to the hospital. He got the lowdown from Cassie and filled me in," Trace explained and reached inside his jacket to the shirt pocket for his cigarettes. "Mind if I smoke?" A negative shake of her head gave him permission, then refused the one he shook from the pack to offer her. "And I spoke to the doctor in the hallway just before I came in."

Another vinyl-covered chair was companionably angled toward his. Pilar sat down in it and leaned earnestly toward him, her dark eyes probing his expression. "What did he say?"

"Probably the same thing he told you." He bent his head to the match flame and puffed on the cigarette, then lifted his head while he shook out the match.

"Elliot's going to recover. He told you that, didn't he?" It was a demand.

As he lowered his hand to toss the burned-out match in an ashtray, Trace noticed that Pilar's hands were clenched into fists on her lap, knuckles showing white. There was a moment when he debated whether to let her believe what she wished or to prepare her for the worst.

"It's too soon to make that kind of judgment." He opted for a middle road that would at least provide a cushion. "The first twenty-four hours after a massive coronary attack such as Elliot's are critical. If he passes that crisis point without another attack, his chances improve. Three days afterward there's another critical period. But either way"—Trace finally looked at her—"it's likely some kind of heart surgery will be needed. Any operation involves risk."

"He'll make it." She was staring at some unseen spot on the floor. "A lot of people have heart attacks and recover to lead normal lives. A year from now Elliot will be jogging again. Today will just seem like a bad dream."

A nurse appeared in the doorway. "Mrs. Santee, your husband is conscious. I think he'd like to see you," she said with a gentle, encouraging smile.

For an instant Pilar was motionless, then

she was squaring her shoulders to gracefully stand. Trace watched the way her lips came together in a smooth, straight line. It seemed to go against her nature to be so controlled.

"You are his son, aren't you?" the nurse inquired. "Perhaps you should come now, too."

Chapter Two

"𝓗e is extremely weak," the nurse cautioned in a hushed tone as she escorted them into the room. "Don't let him try to talk too much or exert himself. I'm afraid I can only allow you a very few moments."

There was an absent nod of understanding by Pilar but the advice seemed to glide right out of her mind. Her whole attention was focused on the man in the bed, a grotesque copy of her husband. She walked slowly to the bed, trying to shut out the sight of all the apparatus around him.

His dark hair was all mussed. Hesitantly she reached out with tentative fingers to smooth it. There seemed to be more strands of silver present than she remembered. At the light touch of her hand his eyes opened.

"Hello, darling." She bent down to press her lips to his cheek but his skin felt cool and odd.

There was fear lurking in his light blue eyes as they clung to her. His mouth moved and some nearly unintelligible sound came out of it. Pilar cast a panicked look at the nurse.

"He's having trouble with his speech, but it's nothing to be worried about now," the nurse assured her.

"Ssh, don't try to talk too much." She managed to smile at him but she was inwardly struggling with this new vulnerability. Elliot had always seemed so indefatigable, invincible almost. Now he was helpless as a baby.

"I love you." Each word was separately spoken. Although badly slurred, Pilar understood them. It reassured her.

"I love you, too, darling." This time the smile came more easily to her.

But his glance was already leaving her and searching out his son, standing discreetly at the foot of the bed to give them a few minutes alone. He grunted out an "A" sound. Pilar had already followed the direction of his glance.

"I think he wants you," she murmured a little resentfully and started to step back from the bed. Then she noticed the puny movement of Elliot's fingers, clawing at the bedsheet in a grasping gesture. When she took hold of his hand, he tried to squeeze it.

"You want me to stay here?" she asked to be sure she'd understood. His eyes slowly closed in an affirmative reply. It was frightening to realize that even that seemed to be an effort to him.

"I'm here, Dad." Trace stood close beside her, their shoulders almost brushing. The perfumed scent of her hair was a sweet incense in the room. "Don't try to talk anymore."

Pilar felt his attempt to lift the hand she held, so she did it for him. His gaze, however, continued to cling to his son's face. "Take . . . care . . . of . . . her."

The significance of his request escaped Pilar for the span of a few seconds. When the inherent finality in his words hit her, she threw an accusing look at his son, as if he were somehow to blame for Elliot giving up. There was a long moment when Trace neither looked at her nor responded to the request. Reluctance seemed to claim him as a muscle in his jaw flexed convulsively.

"I will," he said finally and slid a half-screened look at her, measuring her reaction.

An angry protest seethed through her system. Tightly she held on to Elliot's hand when it went limp. "Don't be silly, Elliot." Her chiding voice was falsely light and she had to force it through her teeth. "You're going to get better. I'm not going to let you go, so you have no choice."

There was an attempt at a smile as the corners of his mouth twitched weakly. "You . . . no . . . say." Only three words could she understand, but the resignation that seemed to be in his expression was sufficient to make it clear. Elliot was conceding the outcome.

"You aren't going to die!" The low pitch of her voice was taut and vibrating with forceful rejection. "Do you hear me, Elliot?" There was the smallest nod of his head for an answer, then the nurse was touching her arm and issuing a warning shake of her head.

"You'll have to leave now so he can get some rest," she advised them in a soft undertone.

Reluctantly Pilar let go of her husband's hand and turned to plead with the nurse for compassion. "Please, may I just sit with him?" It was difficult to be humble when all her impulses wanted to make demands.

"I'm sorry, no." The firm refusal was tempered with a gentle sympathy. "I'm afraid it's doctor's orders."

Before Pilar could argue the unfairness of them, a pair of large hands fitted themselves to her shoulders. "We understand." Trace Santee's voice came quietly in response and undermined any argument she might have put forth.

The guiding pressure of his hands turned her away from the nurse toward the door. Pilar glanced over her shoulder for one last glimpse of Elliot. His eyes were closed but reassuring beeps were coming from the machines monitoring his vital signs.

Her shoulders were released but it was a mere shifting of contact as an arm curved itself to her back, his fingers lightly gripping the lower rib cage. The latent strength that seemed to emanate from his touch was offensive to Pilar, a cruel and physical reminder of how pitifully weak her husband was. That Trace Santee was of Elliot's flesh and blood made it even harder to bear.

The warmth of her flesh seemed to heat his hand, but the rigidity of her carriage was its own kind of rejection. Regardless of how distraught she might be about his father, her body signals discouraged any attempt at familiarity by him. It put his teeth on edge. In the hallway Trace let his arm slide away.

"He'll rest for a while," he announced, quietly inspecting her profile, so tense yet expressionless. "It's a good time for us to go to the cafeteria and get a bite to eat. I don't know about you, but I haven't had anything since lunch."

"No, thank you. You go ahead," she refused and moved away from him to the waiting room.

For a long moment he watched the natural sway of her hips as she walked from him. It was a graceful movement, yet so subtly provocative. His jaw hardened as he tossed a half-glance over his shoulder at the hospital room door and cursed himself for allowing his thoughts to take that wayward direction. His father was lying in that room and he was standing out here coveting his wife. A bitter, black bile seemed to coat his tongue. Trace turned abruptly, long crisp strides carrying him away from the waiting room.

Twenty minutes later he returned with a cup of sweet, black coffee for his father's wife.

A family acquaintance was with her. She thanked him for the coffee, but Trace noticed that she didn't touch it.

Through the course of the early-evening hours several friends came by. None of them stayed long, speaking a few minutes with Pilar or himself and offering any assistance the Santees might need at this particular time.

By nine o'clock it was just the two of them again. Trace took his time crushing out a cigarette in the ashtray, half filled with smoked butts. When his glance ran to her, she stood up and restlessly paced to the window.

"What time are you planning to go home?" Trace studied her through eyes that were half closed to mask the closeness of his interest.

"I'm not." There was nothing to see beyond the darkened window and Pilar turned away from it, absently rubbing the stiff muscles in her neck, knotted with tension. "You can leave whenever you like. Cassie will be there to let you in. I'm going to stay here tonight."

"Why?"

Her dark gaze shot to him, irritation simmering in their black brilliance. "So I can be here in case . . . Elliot calls for me."

The question hardly warranted an answer. She avoided the lazy probe of those gray eyes, too rawly conscious of the unreasoning dislike that had sprung up for the healthy son of her dangerously ill husband. There was a vague, nagging wish that he was the one in that hospital bed instead of Elliot, which only added to her feelings of guilt.

"You need a good night's rest as much as he does." His head was tipped slightly back, its angle suggesting a challenge that his voice hadn't carried.

"If I get tired, I'll curl up in one of the chairs," Pilar retorted. "I know Elliot asked you to take care of me, but I'm more than capable of taking care of myself. There's no need for you to be concerned about my well-being." That bedside request had only added to her building resentment of this son of Elliot's.

He rolled to his feet in a leisurely slow fashion and ambled across the room to stand in front of her, his thumbs hooked in the hip pockets of his smooth-fitting denim pants. All that lazy male indolence made her bristle. She ached inside, hurting so much that lashing out in anger seemed her only means of vocalizing this pain and fear.

"Maybe you'd like to explain how long you'll be able to function on sheer nerve alone," he murmured. "That's all that's keeping you going now. No food today. No sleep tonight."

"I think that's my problem." Her chin lifted a fraction higher, exposing more of the magnolia-smooth curve of her throat.

"Are you trying to impress someone with a devoted-wife act?" He cocked his head to the side, measuring her with a dry glance. "No one but the hospital staff is going to witness your all-night vigil. All of Elliot's friends are home. Or are you doing it because you think it proves you love him?"

"I'm not staying for anyone's benefit except my own," she flared with indignation. "I want to be close by him."

"Staying here tonight won't do him any good—or you any good," he countered, unmoved by the cutting edge of her voice. "If he recovers from this attack, there will come a time when he'll need every bit of your strength. Exhausting yourself now won't help him later."

It was very difficult to argue with his logic. Pilar wavered indecisively, a darkly troubled glance straying in the direction of Elliot's room, blocked from her view by intervening hospital walls.

No matter how superstitious it sounded, she couldn't help wondering if Elliot might not have suffered that attack if she'd gone with him to play tennis. And it was a different face of that same superstition that insisted she stay at the hospital if she didn't want something else to happen to Elliot. In the light of his son's argument her reason sounded crazy and childish.

"The hospital will call if there is any change in his condition." Trace added a further argument while he watched her struggling to make up her mind.

"All right." Pilar gave in, refusing to be ruled by ridiculous superstition.

* * *

The imposing two-and-a-half-story house was a white blue in the night's darkness, surrounded by gardened lawns shaded by live oaks draped with ghostly Spanish moss. Its architecture was generally considered as fairly typical of the southern planter style, with a porch circumventing the house on three sides and supporting a balcony above it, protected by the wide overhang of the house's slanting roof.

In its history it had gone by many names. The first Mrs. Santee had resurrected the name of Dragon Walk, given to it by one of its previous owners, an amateur archaeologist. The chain of steep loess hills, which stretched northward from Natchez to Vicksburg, were fossil-rich in the skeletal remains of mastodons and giant sloths, mammoth prehistoric beasts upon which the dragon myth was based. The old plantation home was located in these hills on the northern edge of Natchez, hence its colorful name, Dragon Walk.

When the car turned into the carriage-wide driveway, the front porchlight came on. It was a welcoming touch and Pilar experienced a moment's relief that she wasn't going home to an empty house. Cassie Douglas was there to fill the large, rambling home with her warmth. Pilar stopped the car at the head of the circular drive and reached for her purse in the middle of the front seat.

"Do you want me to put the car away for you?" The inquiry came from the shadowy figure sitting in the front passenger seat. During the ride from the hospital their conversation had been desultory at best.

"No. I'm leaving it here in case the hospital calls in the night." The interior light flashed on when she opened the car door, giving her side vision a glimpse of the craggy planes of his sun-browned face.

The slam of the passenger door echoed the closing of her side door. She paused to adjust the knotted sleeves of the lavender sweater tied loosely around her neck while he pulled his duffel bag from the rear seat. There was a chilling coolness in the air, fragrant with the sweet scent of gardenias.

Dragon Walk was famous for its floral gardens and flowering trees. Something was always in bloom year-round. Gardenias and camelias in the winter, azaleas and crocuses in the spring, roses and water lilies in the summer, and a profusion of chrysanthemums in the fall.

After sliding an absent glance in Trace's direction to assure that he was coming, Pilar followed the short sidewalk to the fanned steps rising to the wooden porch. The upright pillars supporting the porch roof and second-floor balcony were carved from the trunks of cypress trees and layered smooth with coats of white paint.

White wicker chairs, sofas, and tables extended the living area of the large house onto the porch, with some of the hardier potted plants left outside to add life. The exposure of the porch on three sides of the house insured that there would always be a place to enjoy a breeze in summer's sultry season or sunshine during winter's cooler days. It was one of the most frequently used areas of the house.

Her heels made clicking sounds on the gray porch decking as Pilar crossed to the massive, solid mahogany door, nearly three inches thick. Before she reached it, the ornate brass knob was turned from the inside and the door swung inward. She smiled wanly at the tall, straight black woman waiting to greet her.

"Hello, Cassie," she said.

"I've been worried about you," Cassie Douglas announced with faint reproval. In her middle fifties, nearly the same age as Elliot, she had few lines in her coffee-colored skin to reveal the accumulation of years. The silver that salted the soft black curls framing her proud features appeared to be the artful work of the best hairstylist. "I was sure you were going to get some wild notion in your head to stay at the hospital all night."

"She did, but I talked her out of it." Trace walked into the house behind Pilar and swung the duffel bag off his shoulder to hang at his side. He hooked an arm around the woman's trim waist and pulled her close to plant a kiss on a smooth cheek. His gray eyes glittered with a rakish light. "How's my favorite southern belle?"

"Don't you go using your flattery on me, Trace Santee. It never got you anywhere when you were a boy and it won't now." She mocked the expansiveness of his compliment even while she hugged an arm around his middle. "I talked to Digger after he left you off at the hospital, so I knew you'd be here tonight. I've got your room all ready, and I baked you my own special recipe for pecan carrot cake. It's out in the kitchen along with a pot of fresh coffee."

"I suppose I've got to promise to behave myself before you'll give me a piece," he teased.

"It wouldn't do any good. I swear you were born looking for trouble," she declared with a trace of regret. More than most, Cassie knew how much trouble he'd found.

Dragon Walk had been her home for the last twenty-six years. A highly intelligent woman, Cassie Douglas was a licensed practical nurse. She'd come to work for the family when Trace's mother, the first Mrs. Santee, had contracted multiple sclerosis, a degenerative muscle disease. Trace was only eleven when his mother passed away, and Cassie had stayed on to look after him.

Yet, all the while she served in the role of housekeeper and cook, she never gave up her career. She constantly took refresher courses to keep abreast of medical advancements and new procedures, and took other home cases on a day-work basis. And she'd kept a house of her own, what had been the overseer's cottage on Dragon Walk, and raised a family of three children.

Her late husband had been a riverman,

working the docks and the barges. Trace remembered little about him except that Ogden Douglas had introduced him to the river life. Looking back, Trace marveled at the way Cassie had managed to accomplish so much —something he'd been too young to appreciate at the time.

"You're as bad as Oggie, coming straight off the river—and smelling like it, too." Always immaculate herself, she ran a critical eye over his appearance, but there was a softness in her eyes, tender with memories of her husband. "I'm surprised they didn't kick you out of the hospital for fear you'd contaminate something. You need a bath and a change of clothes."

"Not as much as I need that coffee and cake in the kitchen," Trace insisted with a lazy smile, then slid a half-glance at Pilar. "Don't you think you could use some, too?"

Since her marriage to Elliot, Pilar had become very close to Cassie. As she had observed the reunion, there had been an odd feeling of jealousy at the open display of affection and deep closeness. Considering Elliot's precarious condition, they seemed much too happy and uncaring for her liking.

"No." She addressed Cassie. "I wanted to bring you up to date on Elliot." She was sternly sober, inserting his name into the conversation to remind them why they were standing there at this hour of the night.

"There's no need," Cassie informed her gently. "My daughter, Melissa, is a nurse on the maternity ward at the hospital. She's been checking in with me regularly since she went on duty this afternoon, so I have the inside story on how he's doing."

"I see," Pilar murmured stiffly and lowered her gaze. "If you'll excuse me, I'm going upstairs. There've been so many people at the hospital, I'd just like to be alone for a while."

The front stairwell doubled back on itself to climb to the second floor of the house. Both Trace and Cassie silently observed her departure until she rounded the landing to go up the second flight. The imported crystal chandelier suspended from the ceiling of the large foyer gleamed on the polished mahogany railing that zagged up the stairwell.

A long, troubled sigh came from Cassie, drawing Trace's glance to her as she started toward the kitchen. "I don't like to see her that way—all held in. I had a feeling they were too happy, that some kind of crash had to happen. You should have seen the two of them together." She smiled absently, remembering. "They were always holding hands and snuggling on the sofa. Every day was a honeymoon. Your father saw to that. She's a sensible, practical girl, but he kept her caught up in a romantic dream, all soft lights and violins. I think he was afraid she'd stop loving him if he didn't court her every minute."

"It might be a good idea if you fix a tray and take it up to her later," Trace suggested. "She didn't eat anything at the hospital."

As she pushed open the door to the kitchen,

she gave him a wry glance. "You still don't talk much, but you manage to say a lot. Sometimes I find it hard to believe you're a southern boy."

"You do enough talking for both of us, Cassie," he countered dryly.

Talking was a favorite southern pastime, engaged in by most of its native sons and daughters, but Trace was not loquacious by nature. There were a lot of situations he probably could have talked himself out of if he'd tried.

"And there's some things a woman has an instinct for knowing without being told. Those things I keep to myself." It was a rather enigmatic comment that created an opening in the conversation, but he chose not to fill it.

He lowered his long frame into one of the high-backed wooden chairs around the cloth-covered table while Cassie sliced him a large piece of the frosted cake and poured each of them a cup of coffee.

"Have you spoken to Cal lately?" Trace asked, referring to her son. "I looked him up the last time I was in New Orleans a couple of weeks ago. That's quite a new grandbaby you have."

The conversation drifted around her family. Cassie did most of the talking while Trace ate his cake and washed it down with the strong black coffee. Cassie was never idle for long, preparing a small plate of sandwiches to take up to Pilar in between sips of coffee and the never-ending dialogue. When she had finished with her family, she started bringing him up to date on some of his old friends.

"You're a terrible gossip, Cassie," he declared with a smiling shake of his head at the extent of her information and carried his plate and cup to the sink.

"My mother told me long ago that she had no use for gossip." An amused glint appeared in her eyes. "She was absolutely right. The minute I get it, I just pass it on to the first person I see. It isn't worth keeping to yourself." She picked up the tray she'd fixed for Pilar. "I'll just run this upstairs."

"I'll come along with you." He moved ahead of her to open the kitchen door. "It might turn out to be a long night, so I think I'd better get some sleep while I can."

Accustomed to snatching sleep at odd hours, Trace had problems dozing off that night. He tried to blame it on the absence of the thundering engines of a towboat vibrating his bed, pretending that he slept so lightly because of the stillness of the house, the slightest noise disturbing him. There were plenty of small noises that night.

His old bedroom was located next to the master suite. The floorboards creaked with each movement of that room's prowling occupant. Three times in the night he heard the muted sound of the telephone being dialed. It didn't take much guesswork to realize that Pilar was checking with the hospital.

The house was quiet when he wakened to the rosy sunlight streaking through his windows around six in the morning. For another fifteen minutes he lay in bed, smoking that first cigarette and staring at the ceiling. After he'd showered, shaved, and dressed, he went into the wide hallway and started for the stairwell.

The door of the master bedroom stood open, inviting his glance into the room. The satin coverlet was turned back on the canopied bed, but there was no evidence that the bed had been slept in. Trace paused in the hallway, then took a step into the room and searched it with a sweeping glance.

Pilar was awkwardly curled into a narrow loveseat, sound asleep with her hands pillowed under her head. The sight of her pulled him into the room. Her long, sleek black hair tumbled in a rippling tide over her bare shoulders. The rose-colored satin of her nightgown followed the shape of her body, the roundness of her hips, and the slim length of her legs.

An empty milk glass sat on the coffee table in front of the sofa, but a bite had been taken out of only one of the sandwiches on the plate. The line of his mouth thinned. His look ran back to her sleeping face. Her cheek was smooth, no telltale streaks of tears marring its classical line. She appeared to be huddled in a ball for warmth.

After a second's hesitation Trace crossed to the bed and removed the coverlet. Taking care not to disturb the sleep she so badly needed, he draped the satin quilt over her. But the soft weight of it seemed to jerk her awake. The instant she saw him standing by the loveseat, she sat bolt upright, stiff and braced for the worst.

"Oh, my God, the hospital called." The words came out in a quick rush of breath. "Elliot. He's—"

"No. The hospital didn't call." Trace quickly squashed that fear and watched her sag limply against the corner of the loveseat. Her hand lifted to tiredly comb the weight of her black hair away from her face.

"When I saw you . . . I thought . . ." Her confusion faded into a frown as her puzzled gaze searched his face. "What did you want?"

"Nothing." His glance slipped downward to the buttonlike impressions the nipples of her breasts made in the satin material of her nightgown. She seemed unconscious of the fact, not fully awake to be aware of the revealing state of her nightclothes. "When I walked by your room, I noticed the bed was empty."

Pilar glanced at the bed, a forlorn light in her eyes. "I . . . just couldn't sleep in it alone," she admitted in a soft, anguished voice.

Belatedly she realized the coverlet that belonged on the bed was draped on her legs. She lifted a corner of it, trying to remember whether she'd taken it from the bed.

Trace read her bewilderment. "You looked cold." His mouth slanted in a rueful line. "I didn't mean to waken you."

Reaching out, she picked up the small, gold-cased alarm clock sitting on the coffee table to check the time. "It doesn't matter." She lifted the coverlet aside to swing her bare feet onto the floor. "I wanted to go to the hospital early this morning anyway."

"Pilar." He took a step to intercept her when she started for the dressing room.

Halting, she swung around to face him with a blankly questioning look. From the perfect sweep of her eyebrows to the arch of her cheekbones and the soft shape of her lips, she was incredibly beautiful. For an instant Trace was absolutely still.

Then his hands lightly stroked the bareness of her upper arms. "I'll have breakfast ready when you come down. This morning you're going to eat."

"Yes." She agreed without an argument and rubbed a finger on a point in the center of her forehead. "It's probably hunger that gave me this headache."

With an indifferent turn of her body she walked out of his loose hold. For a second longer his hands remained poised in the air where she had been, then slowly closed and came down to his side.

Chapter Three

On the morning of the third day after Elliot's heart attack, the consulting specialist sat down with Pilar and Trace in a corner of the waiting room to discuss his new patient with them. Although he sounded pleased with the way Elliot's condition had apparently stabilized, he refused to be optimistic about his chances for a full recovery.

"At this point we simply can't be sure how much damage his heart has suffered. Until we know"—he lifted his hands in a palm-upward gesture—"we'll simply have to wait and see."

"It's all so frustrating." Pilar's hands were balled into agitated fists of protest.

"I know." The physician appeared regretful

that he couldn't be more specific in his prognosis, but there was an eagerness in the way he pushed his hands on his knees. "If there aren't any more questions, I'll get back to my rounds."

"I have just one request." Trace spoke up to delay the man's departure. "Mrs. Santee has been having trouble sleeping at night. Perhaps you could give her a prescription for some sleeping tablets."

Her mouth opened to protest as the doctor's inspecting glance swept the faint blue circles under her dark eyes. "I'll leave some at the nurse's station for you. We can't have you collapsing from exhaustion."

"It really isn't necessary."

"It's no trouble at all," he assured her and patted her hand before bustling out of the room.

It was true that she'd barely been able to sleep at all the past two nights—and the lack of sleep made her irritable. Knowing these things, Pilar was determined not to let them color her reaction.

"I know you're just trying to be helpful," she addressed Elliot's son with a forced calm. "But if you had said something to me before you spoke to the doctor, I could have told you that sleeping pills don't work. I've tried them before."

"Then take twice the dosage," Trace replied. "Maybe you don't mind being deprived of a full night's rest, but I do. It's been very difficult for me to sleep with you prowling the house until the wee small hours of the morning."

"Maybe you should take the sleeping pills," Pilar retorted.

"Maybe I should," he agreed with a mild shrug.

Instantly she regretted being so sharp with him. "I'm sorry." It was a stiff apology. "I hadn't realized I was disturbing your sleep."

"It's extremely difficult not to be aware of you moving about in the next room, Pilar." Dryness rustled through his voice, its tone seeming to put another meaning to his remark. Wariness flickered briefly through her before she dismissed it.

That evening, when she retired to the master bedroom for the night, the envelope of pills was sitting on her bedside table next to a glass of water. The instructions said to take one pill as needed. Pilar hesitated, then shook two from the envelope into the palm of her hand and washed them down her throat with water from the glass. She crawled into the bed, which seemed so large and empty without Elliot.

Her dark eyes were wide and staring as she lay on her side. It seemed a very long time before the tension in her body began to dissolve. Her eyelids grew heavy; she closed them, just for a minute, then remembered nothing else as she sank into a black, dreamless void.

In the next room Trace crumpled the empty pack of cigarettes and irritably threw it back on the bedstand. The silence was worse than the faint noises. He swung his legs out of bed to sit on the edge of it, his fingers digging into the mattress. The luminous hands on the clock dial showed the hour to be one thirty in the morning.

His shirt was draped over the back of a straight chair in the corner, an extra pack of cigarettes in the front pocket. Trace pushed off the bed and padded across the dark room, clad only in his Jockey shorts. After rummaging until he located the pack, he walked back to the bed, tearing off the cellophane wrapper around the pack.

With the first ring of the telephone, Trace grabbed for the receiver to choke off the sound before it wakened Pilar. He paused a beat, then carried the receiver to his ear.

"Santee residence," he said, then listened to the voice on the other end of the line for a long, long while. He leaned an elbow on his knee and began to rub his forehead, pressing hard. "Yes. Yes, thank you. I'll make the necessary arrangements."

In a slow, halting motion he replaced the telephone receiver on its cradle, then rubbed his face as if trying to wake from a bad dream. His hand trembled when he reached for the pack of cigarettes he'd just opened and left on the bedstand. He lit one, but the lump in his throat wouldn't allow him to inhale the smoke. It billowed out from his mouth, rising to sting his eyes.

Her eyelids seemed so heavy when she tried to open them. Some kind of bright light was shining somewhere. Pilar attempted to roll onto her back, but her body felt weighted and thick. Her eyelashes finally dragged themselves apart. The room was filled with sunlight.

The sleeping pills had worked their magic after all. All her senses felt dull. The thought of Elliot prodded her into moving even though she wanted to do nothing more energetic than shut her eyes again. She fumbled for the clock on the antique bedstand and raised herself up on one elbow with an effort. A groan of dismay came from her throat when she saw that it was past nine o'clock.

The covers were thrown aside as she made a swiveling turn to sit on the edge of the bed. The drug-worn feeling made her pause to gather her wits. When she looked up, Pilar noticed Trace half sprawled in an armchair near the bed.

"Why did you let me sleep so late?" she complained in irritation and lifted a hand to the dull throb in her head. "I'll never make it to the hospital in time to speak to the doctor when he makes his morning rounds."

A small frown marred the smoothness of her forehead as Pilar absently brushed a hand over her mane of thick black hair and impatiently rose to her feet. The matching robe to her rose-satin nightgown was lying across the foot of the bed. She reached for it.

"There's no need for you to go to the hospital today." The low and flat announcement by Trace seemed to freeze her with its ominous undertones.

Her fingers curled into the slick material of her robe, clutching it in front of her. With a turn of her head, Pilar stared at him, her eyes rounded and searching.

"What do you mean?" Pilar demanded in a low rush, her body taut.

He sat forward, drawing his legs up under him and leaning his arms on his thighs. There was a moment when he avoided her gaze and studied the roughness of his sun-browned hands. His thick, shaggy hair was rumpled, shining ebony-black in the sunlight that poured into the room.

"Elliot . . ." Trace paused to look at her. There were no easy words. ". . . had another heart attack in the night." He let that statement settle in before he grimly continued. "They weren't able to revive him."

"No." It was a small sound as she backed away from him, her head slowly moving from side to side in a rejection of his words. Shock had drained much of the color from her face. "You're lying. It isn't true." The denial came quickly, her tone of voice frightened and half angry. She whirled around and grabbed for the telephone at her bedside in a desperate attempt to prove it wasn't true.

In a single, fluid action Trace was out of the

chair and crossing the few feet that separated
them. His fingers dug into the soft flesh of her
upper arm to pull her around to face him
while he wrenched the receiver from her
hand. Her head was thrown back, long hair
spilling down her back in ropes of black silk.
Her arms were stiffly bent in resistance to his
hold, her hands clenched into taut fists.

"Don't put yourself through this, Pilar," he
insisted roughly.

"There's been some sort of mistake," she
declared and attempted to twist away from
him to reach the phone again.

"There's no mistake. I took the phone call
myself. Elliot was officially pronounced dead
at one twenty-five this morning." Trace bluntly pushed the cold facts at her and forced her
to accept the truth.

"You're lying!" Her teeth were bared to
clamp down on the wretched pain.

Impatience shattered the attempt at gentle
reasoning. "He was my father! Why would I
lie about something like this?" Trace demanded, in rough anger at her persistent refusal to
believe him.

For a long agony of seconds she stared at
him, her dark eyes reflecting the awful pain
and grief that were trapped inside. Her
clenched hands loosened to curl her fingers
into his shirt as if needing to cling to something. Trace understood that raw, inexpressi-
ble anguish. He wanted to hold her close and
let the warmth of her body assuage some of
his hurt while he absorbed some of her pain.

The touch of his hands became protectively gentle.

"The hospital called?" Her soft voice sounded dazed and weak.

"Yes, around one thirty this morning." He slowly nodded a confirmation.

"But . . . I didn't hear the phone ring." It was a vague protest mixed with confusion.

"You were sleeping too soundly." Trace let his hands glide to her pale shoulders and down her back onto the satin material of her gown.

Her chin dipped as her breath came quick and deep. All she could see was the front of his shirt, but she wasn't looking at anything.

"It was those damned sleeping pills. I never should have taken them," Pilar declared bitterly. Her head lifted so she could glare accusingly at that roughly virile face, tormented by this painful regret on top of her intense grief. "Why did I listen to you?"

"You needed to rest."

But she wasn't interested in his answer. Her thoughts were too disjointed, flitting from one thing to the next in a subconscious desire to avoid dealing with the reality of Elliot's death.

"Why didn't you wake me up when they called from the hospital?" Pilar was unconsciously trying to blame someone. "I should have known about it right away. You had no right to keep it from me!"

"There was nothing you could have done. Telling you right away wouldn't have changed anything. He was already gone when they called. I—" The dark thick brows came together. Trace was vaguely troubled by the decision he'd made in the early-morning hours, but his motive had been simply to spare her the pain and grief for a little while. "I didn't think it was necessary to wake you and ruin the one good night's sleep you'd had."

"How dare you make that kind of decision for me!" Pilar raged with hurt. There seemed no release for it. Her eyes were so dry, they ached like all the rest of her—one mighty throb.

With a violent shove, she pushed away from him and turned. She found herself facing the antique rosewood bedstand. Her glance fell on the small envelope containing the few days' supply of sleeping tablets. Pilar scooped it up and hurled the hateful thing into the brass-plated wastebasket. Then she stood rigid and motionless, so brittle that she felt like an eggshell that might shatter to pieces at the slightest jar.

"I'm sorry." Trace's husky male voice murmured the words.

At the light touch of his hands on her shoulders, Pilar stiffened still more and extended her arms from her sides, fingers spread wide.

"Don't touch me." Her voice was hoarse, rasping from the well of her agonizing grief. "Just go away and leave me alone." It was a low and insistent demand for privacy.

Trace took his hands away, but he was

reluctant to comply with her second request. There had not been a tear, nor a single outcry of grief. Too much emotion was being suppressed. It was unnatural to be so controlled. This containment of her feelings bothered Trace more than a hysterical outpouring.

"I've already made preliminary arrangements for the funeral services to be held the day after tomorrow, pending your approval." He tried to press the reality of his father's death onto her, but there was no reaction. "You'll need to speak to the funeral director later on to let him know where you'd like Elliot to be buried. It was a question I didn't feel I could answer for you, since I wasn't sure if you wanted him buried in the family plot next to my mother or whether you preferred a different gravesite."

"Get out!" She choked on a hacking sob as terrible shudders racked her shoulders. A spinning pool of pain swirled around her. Pilar never heard the door close behind him when Trace left the room. It was the worst kind of crying—the type with no tears to wash away the awful ache.

The black wreath brushed against the mahogany front door as Pilar closed it on the last of the departing mourners. She paused to switch off the porch light, then turned to walk to the former parlor of the old house. Cassie was just leaving the room, carrying a tray of dirty cups and glasses.

"I'm just carrying these out to the kitchen," she assured Pilar. "We'll leave the cleaning-up until tomorrow morning."

Satisfied that Cassie did not intend to do any more than clear away the dirty dishes, Pilar merely nodded a silent agreement with her plan and continued into the high-ceilinged parlor with its ornate moldings dominated by a chandelier. A smattering of antiques lent an air of authenticity to the room's furnishings.

The clatter of ice cubes in a crystal glass drew Pilar's glance to the side table where Trace Santee was standing. A black arm band encircled the sleeve of the dark jacket he was wearing. The suit and tie took away the ruffi-an look that had always made him seem coarse and uncultured to her. There was a polished, experienced air about him that re-minded her of Elliot even if the physical re-semblance to his father wasn't there.

Trace picked up two glasses and crossed the room to hand one of them to her. While he sipped at the iced bourbon, his gray glance studied her over the rim of his glass. Although it wasn't strictly necessary, she had elected to wear a plain black dress, chicly simple in style. Her neck and wrists were devoid of any jewelry; only the wedding ring adorned her fingers.

Her black hair was skinned away from her face and coiled in a sleek twist on the back of her head. Only a woman with Pilar's striking-ly classical features could get away with such a severe style and still appear beautiful. The haunting shadows in her eyes appealed to him with the vulnerability they indicated. She was a picture of black and white perfection, from the jet-blackness of her hair, eyes, and dress to the marble-white of her skin.

The neat liquor burned her throat, making her cough, but the heat that coursed through her body took away some of the dead sensation. She wandered over to the fireplace with its mantel of Italian marble. Logs were stacked on the andirons in preparation for a fire that had never been lit. She rolled the glass between her hands, the precious metal of her wedding ring clinking against the crystal.

"We were going to bring down all the Christmas decorations from the attic this weekend," she recalled absently.

"I can carry them down for you tomorrow," Trace said.

"No." She turned from the mantel, which would have been bedecked with garlands of holly in another week. The drink glass was clammy and cold with moisture. Pilar set it onto an empty coaster, not liking the feel of it, and rubbed her hands over the snug-fitting long sleeves of her dress as if needing warmth. "I don't think I'll be wanting to celebrate Christmas this year."

"I suppose not." He swirled the cubes in the amber-colored liquor and watched their spinning.

Pilar looked up to the brilliant chandelier, the dangling crystals multiplying the light

from its candle-bulbs. She blinked her eyes in
an effort to ease their wretched dryness.
There was such an aching void inside her that
she wanted to cry.

"What's the matter with me?" She murmured the question, then bit at her lip. Turning, she cast a silently beseeching look at
Trace, as if he might be able to provide the
answer. "I'm a woman who's just buried her
husband. I should be crying my eyes out, yet I
haven't shed a tear—not once."

After an initial stillness at her confessional
rush of words, Trace set his glass on the table
next to hers and slowly approached her.
They'd spent the better part of the last three
days together, but this was the first time she'd
shown that she felt any closeness to him
because of what they'd been through.

"Sometimes it hurts too much to cry." His
gray eyes darkened with a gentle light as he
brought his hands up to cup the rounded
points of her shoulders.

For so long, Pilar had been denying herself
the physical comfort so many had attempted
to offer her, rejecting such contact. Now she
was unconsciously seeking it. Her hands
seemed to automatically curve themselves to
his middle. She felt the life flowing in the hard
flesh beneath the jacket material and the heat
of a living body.

"But I want to cry," she insisted, feeling the
many threads of control snapping one by one.
A trembling started, the vibrations growing

stronger until she began to shake visibly with her pain. "Why can't I cry for him?" Her breath was coming in little sobs. "Why can't I cry for myself?" She closed her painfully arid eyes as the dry sobs shook her shoulders. She beat her head against the point of his chin. "Why? Why?"

There was a sudden collapsing of all the bonds of restraint and she swayed into him, letting her head rest against the side of his jaw. The contents of the soothing words he murmured were unimportant; it was the sound of his voice that mattered, and the human arms that held her close. His hands rubbed and stroked her as if trying to massage away the empty ache within.

His body absorbed the shuddering force of her silent crying while the molding pressure of his hands urged her closer. The powerful desire to comfort her was slowly being overridden by the sensation of her firmly round breasts and the slim saddle of her hips imprinting themselves on his flesh. Raw hunger, too long stifled, began to surface with a gnawing strength that ate away at his sense of decency and discretion.

He turned his mouth into the side of her hair near her temple, moving to seek the intimate feel of her skin. It tasted warm and sweet, scented with some elusive fragrance. Her head was tipped back, making it easy for him to follow the patrician curve of her cheekbones down to the corner of her lips.

When his mouth rolled onto them, her lips seemed to soften under the possessive warmth of the contact.

It was a fleeting response, too casual and too indifferent, not at all what he needed to satisfy the urges that had been with him too long. When she would have turned away from his kiss, Trace spread his fingers into her hair and cupped her head between his hands to hold it still.

Shocked by the blatant, driving passion of the hard mouth eating at her lips, Pilar tugged at his forearms and struggled to break away. The protesting sounds from her throat were muffled by the smothering pressure of his kiss. Her heart pounded wildly in panic. One minute she had known only comfort in his arms. There had been nothing to warn her of this aggressively sexual assault. On top of all the emotional torment she'd been through, it seemed too much.

In desperation Pilar clawed at his face with her fingernails. An inch-long set of red lines made parallel tracks in his cheek where her nails had raked at his flesh as he jerked his head away and grabbed at her hand.

With a quick twist, she slipped free of his hold and backed away warily—especially with the steely glitter of his gaze swung back to her. Tentatively she drew the back of her hand across her throbbing lips. She was trembling, but less from fear and more from a bitter anger.

"I was told you had no respect for anything." She was breathing hard. "I never guessed how true that was."

His chest lifted in a deep and visible breath that seemed to wipe all expression from his face. "There's no excuse for my behavior just now," he admitted stiffly. A nerve twitched in his cheek. "So I won't attempt to make one. But believe me—I regret this as much as you do." She had wanted comfort and he had shown her lust. The knowledge disgusted him far more than she knew.

"You regret!" In the face of his irreverent treatment of her, Pilar was outraged by his lack of contrition. "I want you to leave! Now! This very minute!"

There was a second when Pilar thought he would protest being ordered out of the house that had been his home. After surveying her with a long, measuring look, Trace turned on his heel and walked out of the parlor. She heard his footsteps on the stairs, and suddenly her knees felt very weak.

She sank into the nearest chair and pressed a hand to her lips. She could still feel the sensation of his hard, cruel mouth rocking across them, so forceful and demanding. Her eyes began to fill with tears—tears she hadn't been able to cry before, but this time no sobs accompanied her spilling of pain.

When Trace came down the stairs, he was dressed in the same clothes he'd worn the day he arrived, and the duffel bag was on his shoulder. He headed straight for the front door.

"Trace?" Cassie's voice was filled with question. "Where do you think you're going?"

He paused, his glance sliding past her toward the parlor. "I've been away from the river too long. You know how it is, Cassie."

"I know how it is with some, Trace, like my Oggie. But you—you're seeking the danger and excitement of the river for some other reason. It doesn't bring you any peace." She eyed him with a shrewd and knowing look, her glance darting to the two faint red lines on his cheek. "What have you done this time, Trace? You're running again."

"I was born to trouble—you said it yourself," he reminded her with a twisted smile. Then a grimness settled over his features. "He asked me to look after her. I guess you're going to have to do it for me." His thumb caressed her cheek for an instant, then he pulled it away and headed for the front door.

Cassie watched him walk out the door, so tall and straight—and alone. She was troubled for him. Trace had matured into a fine figure of a man, strong and intelligent. The aimless life he led was such a waste.

A heavy sigh came from her when the door closed. She supposed it had been wrong to hope Elliot's death might be good for his son. Slowly she walked to the parlor, wondering if anything would ever turn Trace around and prod him into making something of himself.

When she entered the parlor, Cassie observed Pilar hastily wiping the tears from her cheeks. "Trace has left."

"Yes, I know." Pilar's voice was husky and stiff. "He stayed for the funeral. What more did you expect?" She was brittly flippant and derisive.

"Don't misjudge him," Cassie cautioned. "Trace isn't as shallow as he might seem."

"I'm really not interested in discussing him." She swung away, agitation rippling through her. "It's been a long day. I think I'll go to my room and read for a while."

As Pilar started to leave the room, Cassie noticed the two glasses sitting on a table. "Now where did those come from?" she declared with a trace of exasperation. "I thought I'd carried everything out to the kitchen."

"That one's mine." Pilar picked up the one sitting on the coaster. "I'll take it upstairs with me. Alcohol is supposed to be a depressant. Maybe it will help me get to sleep."

It was a brisk night, typical of early December weather in the South. The long walk into town did nothing to ease the self-derision that hounded Trace. Nor did it erase the memory of the way it felt to hold her in his arms. Just for a little moment he'd gone crazy with wanting her—and that's all it had taken.

A neon sign blinked an invitation from a building just ahead of him. His steps slowed as Trace approached it, pausing to snap the smoldering butt of his cigarette into the gutter. When he walked inside, the air was stale with the smell of beer and tobacco smoke.

It was a small bar, a little dingy, a little

rundown. Most of its patrons were sitting in chairs or on bar stools positioned to give them a view of the television set on a high shelf behind the counter.

The stool at the near end of the counter bar was at a bad angle to the television set, so it was empty. Trace walked over to it and propped his duffel bag against the wooden bar, then climbed onto the stool, digging a hand into a side pocket to lay some money on the countertop.

The bartender backed grudgingly toward him, unwilling to look away from the car chase on television. He threw him a quick glance, then looked back at the screen. "Yeah, what'll it be?"

"A bourbon on ice—and be generous."

The drink was fixed, the money taken and change given, and all the while the bartender's attention remained on the television show. There was some talking among the men in the bar, but it was kept low, and ceased whenever there was any dialogue. None of them paid any attention to Trace, hunched over his drink at the end of the bar.

At the commercial break he ordered another. The first one hadn't even begun to quench the hot fires that burned inside him. He was angry at himself, and that anger turned everything sour. There was a crazy urge to hit something—a wall—anything—as if lashing out would make him feel better.

Familiar theme music began playing to signal the show's end, and everyone in the bar seemed to start talking at once, laughing and ordering drinks. Trace crushed out his third cigarette and resisted the impulse to tell all of them to shut up.

"Pipe down," someone else complained for him. "The news is comin' on."

"I wonder if they'll say anything about Santee gettin' buried today," someone else said.

Trace searched out the man who'd spoken. There was a big, husky man sitting down the counter from him, with two other fellows.

"Did you ever see the gal he was married to?" The middle one grinned. "She is one sexy-looking woman. And just about half his age, too."

"Do you suppose the new widow will have someone to console her in her time of grief?" The first one chortled lasciviously.

"She's got too much class for you, Frank," the third man declared.

"Yeah, Frank." Trace slid off his stool and walked down the bar as the three men turned, startled by his sudden intervention. He stopped in front of the one they called Frank. "She's got too much class for you." His mouth curled into a sneer. "So why don't you just shut up."

"Nobody asked your opinion." The man frowned and started to turn back to face the bar.

Trace never gave him a chance, grabbing him by the arm and throwing a right cross that caught him on the chin. His companion shouted a protest at the unprovoked attack, and Trace made a swing at him, but it glanced off the man's shoulder. He barely managed to duck away from the fist aimed at his face. It clipped a cheekbone.

All his senses were instantly heightened. He could hear his heart pumping and feel the blood pounding through his veins. The rush of air in and out of his lungs was almost a drunken high. There was only one of him and three of them.

Fragments of the fight stayed in his memory —the moment when he'd buried a fist in someone's stomach and felt the hard muscles collapse, the sight of the ring on a man's finger just before it split his lip, the second when a blow reeled him and the floor came rushing up to meet him. Most of the rest of it was mixed up in the grunting sounds of straining bodies, his or somebody else's, and the shouts of patrons above the blare of the television.

The wail of sirens came toward the last. One eye was so swollen he couldn't see out of it, and there was blood in his mouth from his split lip. His legs were getting wobbly and he was having trouble just staying upright. For the moment his body had tuned out all sensation of pain.

Chapter Four

$\int$omeone grabbed him from behind and locked his arms behind his back. Trace relaxed when he saw a couple of uniformed police cornering his three opponents. The voices and confusion were just a loud buzzing in his ears. A pair of handcuffs were locked around his wrists and he was shoved up against the bar. Grateful for the support, Trace slumped against it, his lungs laboring for air.

"All right! All right!" A voice called for order and quiet, piercing Trace's dazed brain with a glimmer of familiarity. "I wanta know who started this." He hadn't the breath to answer, but there were plenty of witnesses to point the finger. A hand grabbed his arm to turn him around. "All right, tough guy. Aww, hell, I might have known it was you," the voice muttered.

Trace had to turn his head way around to focus the eye that wasn't swollen on the man. "Hey, Digger." His mouth curved in a weary smile. "Like old times, eh?" Trace panted between the words.

"Yeah, old times." The aging officer nodded grimly and turned to the barkeeper. "He's good for the damages." Then to the others, "Anybody gonna press charges?"

There was some low grumbling in the background, but no one spoke up. Digger Jones clamped a hand on Trace's arms and pushed him in the direction of the door.

"My gear?" Trace managed to nod his head at the duffel bag on the floor by the bar.

Digger mumbled something under his breath and picked it up. Once they were outside, he removed the handcuffs and waved Trace toward one of the patrol cars, its blue lights flashing.

"Back seat or front?" Trace tried to smile, but his lip was starting to hurt.

"Front," Digger grunted.

After he slid into the passenger side, Trace slumped in the seat, letting it support him. The soreness was beginning, the dull aches turning into painful throbs. He glanced briefly at Digger when he climbed behind the wheel and shut the door.

"You can just drop me off by the waterfront," Trace said and shut his eyes.

"Did you get a good look at that bar when you walked outa there?" Digger Jones demanded.

"No."

"You smashed it up good," Digger assured him on an impatient note. "Dammit, Trace, I thought you'd told me you learned a few things. One of these times you're gonna start a fight and somebody's gonna get bad hurt. It probably won't be you. The bad ones seldom come out on the wrong end of the stick," he muttered angrily as he drove down the street. "But what happens if somebody does get hurt or killed? Did'ja ever think about that?" he hotly challenged Trace. "Did'ja? You could wind up in prison. All right, so maybe you don't give a damn about yourself— but wouldn't you care if you crippled some guy? Wouldn't you care about his family?"

A frown pulled at Trace's forehead as the words hammered at him. "Don't lecture me tonight, Digger."

There was a long run of silence in the car. At each chuckhole and rough patch in the road, Trace's bruised and battered muscles protested the further abuse. He hurt so much, he didn't even want to think—but that had been his intention all along.

"This is a fine mess." Again Digger grumbled his disapproval. "They bury your daddy this afternoon and you damned near get yourself arrested for brawling in some barroom tonight. You've got a fine way of mourning the dead."

"Shut up, Digger." The remark had touched a sore spot.

"Yeah, I'll shut up," Digger agreed roughly. "'Cause I'm just wasting my breath. Look at you—all bloodied up until your momma could hardly recognize you. What have you got to show for all the living you've done? Nothing. And you know what you're going to have tomorrow? Nothing. There's only one way for you to go, Santee—and that's down."

This time the silence lasted. Trace kept his eyes shut and made no reply to Digger's prediction, letting his head rock on the back of the seat with the motion of the traveling car. When it finally rolled to a stop, he roused himself with an effort, pain shooting through every inch of his body. His right eye was completely swollen shut. He reached for the door handle even before he looked at his surroundings.

A huge white structure loomed beside the parked patrol car. It took him half a second to recognize the rear entrance to Dragon Walk as he stepped out of the car.

"Why the hell did you bring me here?" Trace demanded and felt the cut on his lip start to bleed again. "I told you to take me to the waterfront."

"I figured Cassie oughta take a look at you." Digger climbed out of the car. "I'd have taken you to the hospital, but I wanted to save your family the embarrassment of having everyone in town know you were up to your old tricks again." He hitched his pants higher around his waist and glanced at the back door. "The lights are on in the kitchen. I reckon Cassie is still up."

Trace stayed in the shadows and watched his friend walk up to the back door and rap lightly on the frame. It was several long seconds before the door swung open.

"What are you doing here at this time of night, Digger?" Cassie was silhouetted in the light shining from the kitchen. "Something's happened to Trace." She guessed immediately.

"He started a fight in some bar. I got him out of there and brought him along with me. I thought you'd better take a look at him." He jerked his head in Trace's direction.

Before he could say another word, Cassie was anxiously hurrying down the short flight of steps from the rear door and hustling toward the dark form half leaning against the car. Her hand reached for his chin to turn it and give her a better look at his face. She made a clicking sound of dismay with her tongue.

"It isn't as bad as it looks," Trace muttered and impatiently brushed her hand aside.

There was a part of him that wasn't in the mood for solicitous concern. The fight had been a form of self-punishment, both a way to release all the turmoil inside and to scourge its presence. Physical pain was easier to cope with than mental suffering.

"Come inside and we'll get you cleaned up." She was brusque and firm as she took his arm with a strong grip to guide him to the door.

But Trace hung back, his one good eye running a glance at the plantation house. "No. I'm not coming in." It was a subdued refusal, quiet and stiff.

Long adept at putting two and two together, Cassie guessed his reason. "She's gone upstairs to her room, and you're coming into the kitchen with me where there is some light so I can see what you've done to your eye." She was professionally gruff with him, not tolerating any of his nonsense and pride.

This time Trace let her lead him into the house, his legs operating with stiff coordination. Each step seemed to jar some new sore spot and start some part of his body aching. She guided him to the table and sat him in a chair.

"The coffee should still be hot, if you'd like a cup, Digger." Cassie absently offered the invitation while she began to fill a basin with water and gather the items she'd need to treat Trace.

"No thanks. I'm on duty. I'd better head back into town before they start wondering what happened to me." His expression was grim as he sent a look at Trace. "Try not to get into any more trouble before you leave town. The next time I'll have to haul you in."

"I've done enough for one visit," Trace assured the local officer with a trace of bitter irony.

"Look after him, Cassie. Lord knows, he needs it," Digger advised and went out the door, closing it quietly behind him.

Everything was all arranged on the table beside Trace when Cassie finally bent to her task, first gently and thoroughly wiping the blood from his face. "Trace Santee, what am I going to do with you?" She murmured the words, never pausing in her ministrations or letting her attention falter from her actions. "Who'd you pick a fight with? Muhammad Ali? He certainly did a good job messing up your face." She rinsed out the cloth, and the water in the basin turned a murky reddish brown. "I'd hate to see what you did to him."

"Them," he corrected, wincing when the wet cloth touched his face again. "There were three of them. Unfortunately they were all still standing when Digger arrived on the scene."

"Three." Impatience snapped in her dark eyes as she shook her head mildly. "You always did like to go against the odds. The bigger the better. I don't suppose it would do me any good to ask what started it."

"Something they said I didn't like." His whole face felt funny, all swollen and bruised, throbbing with soreness wherever she touched it.

"Something you didn't like, huh?" Her attention remained intent on his face, but the corners of her mouth were pulled grimly down. "It couldn't be that they made some remark about Pilar, could it?" Her hard glance held his wary, one-eyed look for an instant. "It doesn't take much figuring to come up with that guess. Your father was an important man in this town, and she's got the kind of looks men talk about. And some remark about her would be just the thing to spark that romantic streak in you and push you into thinking you had to defend her honor. All your life you've wanted to slay dragons." Her knowledgeable fingers pressed around his eye and pried the lids apart, letting a slit of light in. "That eye looks bad."

"It hurts like hell," Trace said, commenting on it rather than her observation, but he couldn't leave one subject entirely alone. "I guess she has been an item of gossip for quite a while."

"When she first came to Natchez to inventory and reappraise the antiques at Bentley Hall, she created quite a stir." There was a widening flare of Cassie's eyes to indicate that was an understatement. "Hardly anyone thought that someone so young and so beautiful could have any brains—or experience. It was quite a controversy for a while until they learned she had literally been raised in the business. Both of her parents were antique dealers in Virginia, and highly respected, too. The way Pilar tells it, she knew the difference between Belter and Chippendale when she was four. For three years she worked in London for the Sotheby company—that famous one that handles all those art and antique auctions." All the while Cassie was absently rattling on, telling him things he knew and some he didn't, she was getting crushed ice from the ice-maker attachment on the refrigerator and making a cold compress with a clean, damp cloth. "Hold this to your eye."

Gingerly Trace pressed it to the closed eye and felt the frissons of pain at the contact. Cassie noticed the skinned and cut knuckles of his hands and washed away the caking blood on them.

"Of course, Elliot's whirlwind courtship of her really set the town on its ear. There were some that said they weren't surprised she married him, since she obviously loved 'old things.' Thankfully they were too happy to let a lot of gossip bother them. Elliot was sensitive to it, though—for a lot of reasons." Her glance briefly caught his eye during that small hesitation but she didn't pursue that topic. "Their marriage worked well. She took over the administration of the Santee Foundation, which Elliot had never liked," Cassie said, referring to the trust set up by Trace's grandfather to assist in the funding and preservation of historically significant southern landmarks or sites. "Plus she opened up a small antique shop in town, to keep her hand in the trade."

"That must have given him a lot of free time," Trace mused somewhat absently. "The talk on the river has been that most of the company decisions lately have been made by Cunningham."

"Elliot didn't spend as much time at the

office as he used to," Cassie admitted. "But he wasn't coming home to an empty house anymore either." Although the home office for the Santee Line of river barges was located in Natchez, Trace had always worked out of the terminal in New Orleans. The arrangement had conveniently suited his needs. "What about your ribs? Did you get any of them cracked or broken?"

"No." Trace flinched from the probe of her fingers. "They're just bruised." The pounding in his head seemed to increase in intensity. "Have you got any aspirin?"

While Cassie went to the sink to get him a glass of water, Trace managed to light a cigarette despite the stiff soreness of his fingers. But the smoke made the cut on his lip sting painfully, and he put out the cigarette after only one drag.

The muted sound of a car motor penetrated the thick walls of the house. The hairbrush paused in midstroke as Pilar listened, but there wasn't any knock at the front door. After a few minutes she decided someone had driven slowly past the house and resumed brushing out her long hair.

It was only seconds later that she heard a car driving away. Puzzled, she walked to the balcony doors in time to see headlight beams as a car turned onto the road past Dragon Walk. A tiny frown creased her forehead. She tried to shrug it off, telling herself that Cassie had probably spoken to the late callers and indicated that she had retired to her room.

Her room, in the singular. It was no longer "their" room. Melancholy settled over her as she slid the brush onto the marble-topped vanity. After thinking in the plural for so long, it seemed unnatural. Sometimes none of this seemed real. A sudden tightness gripped her throat, trapping a breath.

Elliot. Sweet, gallant Elliot, a fine southern gentleman to the tips of his toes. How many times had she gotten upset over something, yet there had never been a harsh word spoken by him. He had openly adored her, and it had been impossible not to be completely captivated by his romantic charm. Never in her life had she known anyone like him. It was certainly apparent that Trace Santee didn't take after him. The mere thought of him brought a ripple of disgust.

A restless discontent pushed her to the door. She ventured into the hallway with the vague excuse of finding Cassie and discovering who had stopped by a few minutes earlier. All the lights were on downstairs, reflecting their glow into the stairwell.

When she didn't find Cassie in the parlor, Pilar headed for the kitchen. As she opened the door she was looking directly at the man sitting at the table with his back to her. Even though she couldn't see his face, the clothes and the leanly muscled shape of him were enough to give away his identity.

"What are you doing here? I thought I told you—" Her simmering accusal was cut off in midstream as he turned in her direction and lowered the bulky cloth that had covered part of his face.

Practically the whole right side was a swollen, purpling mass of bruised flesh. An open cut puffed the top of his mouth, and there were less severe bruises on the other half of his face, distorting his rugged features.

"My God," Pilar gasped at the brutal sight. "What happened?" She threw a short glance at Cassie, whose mouth was tightly shut in silence; then her questioning gaze darted back to Trace.

His back was turned to her again as he awkwardly straightened to his feet, giving her a narrow side glimpse of his jaw. "I ran into somebody's fist." It was a half-muttered, irritated response.

There was a moment of blankness until his answer finally sunk in. Her lips thinned into a narrow line. "You mean you were in a fight," she retorted in disgust.

"Yes." The clothpack was thrown into the sink.

"I can't believe you are Elliot's son!" Pilar declared in a kind of dumbfounded anger and contempt.

"Pilar—" Cassie attempted to insert a disapproval.

"No." She refused to be silenced. "Maybe you feel sorry for him, but I don't! He's gotten just what he deserves. And I have no pity for him at all."

"I never asked for any!" He half turned to his left, bringing her into his vision.

Her raking glance skimmed his rangy build, the skinned knuckles, and the rumpled black hair. "You really are good for nothing," she stated with a decisive pronouncement. "What do you think you proved by fighting tonight? That you're a man? A tough guy?" she taunted him.

"It proves I'm human!" Trace shot back. "That I've got feelings and hurts the same as you! You're so wrapped up in your own grief that you think you're the only one who cares that he's dead. All right, so maybe I offended you this evening, but all I wanted to do was give comfort and be comforted. It started out all very innocent, but unfortunately I got carried away. When I left this house, I felt about as low and rotten as a man can get! But I don't expect you to understand that. According to you, I don't feel anything!"

The bitterness and suppressed anger in his voice lashed out at her. Pilar didn't retaliate, although her dislike of him continued to glitter in her eyes. Perhaps there was some truth in his explanation even if it didn't justify his behavior.

He swung away from her silence and reached for the duffel bag sitting on a corner of the countertop. "I'm going to borrow your car, Cassie. You can pick it up tomorrow morning under-the-hill."

The slamming of the door vibrated through the kitchen. Pilar unconsciously flinched from the sound but her expression remained hardened against him. She flashed a look at the black woman, standing so silently by the table.

"You think I was wrong for speaking out the way I did, don't you?" Pilar challenged, preferring to air their disagreeing views.

There was a faint shrug of Cassie's shoulders that wouldn't pass judgment. "I know him better than you do. I know the things that are good about him, and I know the things that are bad. He has troubles that you don't know about and I think it's better that way."

"What do you mean?" Pilar frowned at Cassie's deliberate attempt at mystery.

"I mean that you're going to have a hard enough time without taking on any of Trace's problems," she replied. "He'll have to work them out himself. I just hope he does a better job of it than he's done so far."

A fine drizzle fell from the low, murky clouds, instilling a damp chill in the air, but Trace didn't feel it under the bulky thickness of his navy wool sweater and unzipped windbreaker. The deck beneath his feet vibrated with the whine of the engines. Wisps of fog trailed across the surface of the intercoastal waterway, too thin to present any hazard.

There was a single, blaring blast of a towboat's horn, which was echoed by his boat. Straightening from the railing, Trace swung his gaze to the front, beyond the prow of the first barge, and spied the towboat pushing barges toward them. They were riding high in the water, a clear indication that their holds were empty. One blast of the horn signaled the towboat's intention of passing on the port side.

As the tow vessels drew abreast, a smile twitched at the corners of his mouth. A string of multicolored lights circled the pilothouse of the towboat, and an artificial, faded green wreath was tacked onto a large life ring on the side, near the name *Sophie B*. Trace lifted a hand in silent greeting to the man at the controls. Engines throbbed, turning props and churning up water in a muddy wake as the towboats passed.

The faint smile lingered on his face as Trace pivoted to slide an amused glance through the opened window of the wheelhouse at the pilot taking his turn at watch on the *Delta Belle*. "Either the Swede hasn't been sober since Christmas, or else he's getting a headstart on next year."

"I'll ask him." Dan Bledsoe chuckled and picked up the radio mike. There was a crackle of communication over the short-wave before he came back with the answer. "He said he hasn't been home for Santa Claus to visit him. It'll be another week before he gets back. Hope we don't get stuck like that. My wife's due to have her baby the end of the month."

"This is supposed to be a turn-around haul," Trace replied.

"Yeah." There was a skeptical quality in the response. "I've heard that before."

So had Trace, but he wasn't a family man like some of the others on the crew. He didn't complain about the delays in port, or the junk hauls they'd been making recently. He tapped the windowsill in a gesture of decision.

"I'm goin' below. She's all yours."

"Aye, Cap'n," Bledsoe replied absently, already looking ahead at the bend in the channel.

After hours at the wheel negotiating through an early-morning fog and drizzle with one eye on the radar screen and an ear tuned for the blast of a horn, Trace was ready for a break. It hadn't been his watch, but as the senior pilot, he hadn't been willing to let the green Bledsoe take it alone, since he'd only obtained his river pilot's license seven months ago.

A pot of coffee was cradled on a back burner of the stove in the mess cabin. Trace filled a cup and carried it to the table where Evers, the cook, was cheating at a game of solitaire.

"Want something to eat?" Evers chewed out the words through the cigar in his mouth.

"Nope." Trace took off his hat and dropped it on the table while he combed a hand through his hair, then let it rub the knotted muscles in his neck.

"Your mail's still sittin' over there. Ya never did open it," Evers reminded him and slipped an ace from the pile.

"It's just bills." Trace rocked his chair back

to reach the short stack of envelopes with his name on them, then leafed through them, looking at return addresses before bothering to open them.

"What do you suppose is gonna happen to the line now that your old man's gone?" Evers lifted his chin to frown curiously at Trace, the cigar wigwagging from his teeth.

"What do you mean?" He used his pocket-knife to slice open an envelope. An eyebrow arched briefly when he saw the amount listed as damages at the bar where he'd had the fight six weeks ago.

"There's been some speculation that his widow might sell it. I just wondered if you knew." The ash fell off Evers' cigar onto the cards. The cook muttered under his breath and swept it off the table with his hand.

"Could be." Trace shrugged with disinterest.

Evers began flipping down cards again. "Can't imagine a woman running a barge line." He darted an interested look at Trace. "You'd get some of the money if she sold it, wouldn't ya?"

"Mmhmm." It was an affirmative sound as he slid the knife blade under the flap of another envelope. He unfolded the official-looking letter and skimmed the notice of a special stockholders' meeting of the Santee Line, Ltd. Disinterested, Trace shoved it back in the envelope.

"She wouldn't get much for it if she sold it," Evers announced, continuing the conversation whether Trace was interested in the subject or not. "The business has been going downhill the last few years. Equipment's getting older and prices are getting higher."

"There have been too many cheap loads to undesirable ports," Trace acknowledged—undesirable from the standpoint of getting good loads to haul out. "And too much money has been spent on repair and maintenance of equipment that's too old to warrant it."

"Hell, anybody on the river knows that," the cook declared. "But I wouldn't want to take bets on how long it's been since anyone at the main office has been out on these waters. These boats and barges are just numbers on paper to them—and the ports are just places on a map. You let me run this company for a month, and you'd see plenty of changes."

"That's what we all say." Trace's mouth quirked as he drank down his coffee.

"Yeah, I guess so." Evers smiled, too, at his own braggadocio. "It's just talk, and it never amounts to nothing. That's why I'm sittin' here on this vibratin' machine and they're sittin' in some plush office and smokin' five-dollar cigars. They don't make presidents out of river bums."

"Right," Trace agreed absently as he scooped up his mail and fingered the envelope with the notice of the stockholders' meeting.

A chair was pulled out for her at the conference table. Pilar smiled briefly at the attorney before smoothing the back of her navy linen skirt to sit down.

"Thank you, Mr. Forrestown," she murmured.

"I believe you know everyone here," he said.

"Yes, I do." Pilar glanced at the half-dozen men slowly resuming their places at the table now that she was seated.

"I hope you don't object to my inclusion of Mr. Cunningham," the attorney offered respectfully. "I know he isn't a shareholder in the company, but since he's been acting as an interim president, I felt he should be present for this meeting."

"Of course," she agreed and nodded to the squat, balding man sitting across the table from her. "I'm glad you could join us."

Payne Forrestown remained standing. "Since all the directors are present, and the shareholders are represented, either by proxy or their presence, perhaps we should get down to the business of electing officers and appointing a new member to the board." There was a nodding assent around the table. He smiled down at Pilar, slightly patronizing. "We won't be formal about this. Whenever you wish to speak or ask a question, feel free to do so."

"Thank you."

None of them were entirely comfortable with her in the room, and Pilar could feel their restiveness. Many of them clung to the old tradition that kept women and business separate.

"Perhaps we should begin by nominating—" He was interrupted by a knock on the door to the conference room. "Come in," he called out impatiently.

When Trace Santee walked in, Pilar sensed the ripple of surprise that passed through the room. Unlike the other men, dressed in dark business suits and ties, he was wearing a tan windbreaker over a white shirt, opened at the throat.

"Trace, I—" The attorney stopped and glanced down at the papers on the table in front of him. "I didn't realize you were going to attend. I believe I have your proxy right here."

"I believe you're mistaken, Payne." A smooth smile spread across his rugged features, which carried none of the bruises that had marred it the last time Pilar had seen him. "I didn't mail one in."

"I see." But it was obvious that the attorney didn't *see* anything. Trace's appearance had thrown everyone in the room off stride. "You'll have to forgive me. I must have presumed you wouldn't come, since you never have attended any of our previous meetings."

It seemed everyone in the room drew an audible breath when Trace pulled out the chair at the head of the table and sat down. "I haven't," he agreed smoothly. His gray eyes made a slow survey of the men seated at the table and lingered an instant on Pilar. "But I've never owned the company before."

A little shock seemed to vibrate through Pilar. It wasn't possible. According to the will, the bulk of Elliot's shares had come to her.

"In case you haven't counted them lately"— Trace looked straight at her when he spoke— "between the shares my father left me and the ones I received from my mother's estate, I hold the majority of shares in the Santee Line."

"Well, yes . . . that's true." The attorney nodded a dazed confirmation. "But—" He was plainly at a loss for words.

It was not resentment of his ownership that smoldered behind the calm facade Pilar showed him. After all, he was Elliot's son, so it was natural that he should inherit control of the company. It was a distrust of the capricious whims that ruled him, and his lack of respect for the established order of things. She saw the gleam in his gray eyes that issued a challenge and amusement. Trace Santee was enjoying the discomfort he was creating.

"How typical of him," Pilar thought, "to arrive unannounced and throw everyone into confusion—stirring up trouble." She quietly seethed, conscious of the heated tempo of her pulse. He sat crookedly in the chair, a pose of lazy indolence with one arm stretched on the table to idly turn a pencil in a circle.

Cunningham hunched forward in his chair and turned his bald head in the direction of the end chair. "You have never taken any interest in the operation or management of the company before, Trace. Naturally the members of the board are surprised by this apparent turn-around."

"It's been four or five years since the company has issued any dividends to the shareholders." Trace seemed to throw that out as a reason while he eyed the interim president through the tops of thick lashes.

"In the past," Pilar said and heard the huskiness in her voice, "you never bothered to attend any of the previous shareholders' or directors' meetings. This is rather a sudden concern about the financial status of the company, isn't it?"

"But in the past"—he paused, eyeing her steadily, yet with that gleam of mocking amusement that had taken on a harsh note—"my father ran the company, Mrs. Santee."

He picked up the pencil, and tapped the eraser end on the table. The little gesture seemed to draw to a close any further discussion of this subject. The lazy pose was thrown off as he straightened in the chair and rested his forearms and elbows on the table. With the action, the control of the meeting seemed to flow to him.

"I don't know how these procedures are conducted, but"—his cool, challenging gaze swept the table—"maybe we should begin by installing a new president."

The brief silence was broken by the attorney

as he sat down in the empty chair next to Pilar's, relinquishing his authority over the proceedings. Nervously he cleared his throat, conscious that the others were looking to him. "Dale Cunningham has been acting as interim president," he said. "I believe the general opinion has been that the position would become permanent. Elliot thought very highly of his management abilities."

"I have one quarrel with Cunningham taking over as president of the Santee Line," Trace stated, apparently indifferent to the tension in the air. "He hasn't been on the river in twenty years or more. He's lost touch with the business and the changes it's made."

No one commented on his assessment of Cunningham or his lack of endorsement. Payne Forrestown studied the documents on the table in front of him, giving them a pretense of attention, and asked the question no one else wanted to voice. "Is there someone you would like to suggest for the post?"

"Me." The slow smile that spread across the bluntly chiseled features held no humor.

Forty-five minutes after Trace had walked into the conference room, the meeting was concluded. It had been awkward for everyone except Trace. So Pilar wasn't surprised when they all remembered appointments elsewhere and cut short the idle talk that usually followed the formal gatherings.

Pride refused to allow her to join the stampede from the room. There was calm deliberation in the time she took, saying her good-byes to her late husband's business friends while she worked her way slowly to the door. Yet her senses were always alert to Trace, warning her that they would ultimately meet at the door.

The Italian handbag hung from a strap over her shoulder. Pilar paused to put on the black kid gloves, conscious that Trace was finally beside her. Ebony combs swept the midnight sleekness of her hair away from her face and revealed the pearl studs piercing the lobes of her shell-like ears.

"I guess I should thank you for voting for me." The sound of his low voice vibrated over her skin.

"You're welcome," she replied smoothly and kept her gaze downcast while she fitted the soft material between her fingers.

His arm crossed in front of her vision as he leisurely braced a hand against the wall and blocked her path to the door. Her glance made a darting lift to his face before she returned to the task of drawing on the other glove.

"Everyone waited to follow your lead. With their support, you could have made a fight of it," he pointed out, tilting his head downward and to one side to probe curiously at her expression.

"You obviously came looking for trouble. I'm sorry I disappointed you." She arched him a cool smile, aware of the straining tautness of her nerves.

His earthy virility was a physical presence in front of her, the bronzed column of his throat and the wisps of chest hairs springing into view where his shirt collar was unbuttoned. She was conscious of his rough good looks and the firm line of his mouth. There was a thready awareness that she missed the contact with a man's body—Elliot's body.

"I don't think you're sorry," he mused.

"Does it matter?" Pilar countered with forced indifference. "You own the majority stock. And you're Elliot's son, so why shouldn't you take over now that he's gone?" It was her reason for not attempting to block his takeover of control. "Besides, as you pointed out, the company hasn't been paying any dividends, so I didn't have anything to lose."

"That's true." But his eyes continued to probe.

"The company is yours to do with as you wish." There was a curtness in her voice. "That's what you wanted. I don't know what you intend to do with it—probably ruin it the way you've blackened everything else in your life. I'm sure you tore all your toys apart when you were a child. Now you have a bigger toy that you can destroy. I don't particularly care."

His jaw hardened at her coolly aloof condemnation. He made an unhurried push away from the wall and shifted out of her path to the door. "I'm going to be making a lot of trips back and forth between Natchez and New

Orleans these next few months. I'm sure you'll understand if I'm too busy to call on you when I'm in town."

"Of course." Briefly Pilar inclined her head, nodding to him before she moved smoothly to the door. Her flesh tingled with the sensation of his gaze, observing her departure.

Chapter Five

$\mathscr{T}$he cuffs of the white shirt were rolled halfway back on his forearms. The dove-gray jacket to his suit was hooked on a finger and slung over his shoulder, a multistriped gray tie sticking out of a side pocket. The top buttons of his shirt were unfastened to invite the evening breeze onto his damp skin.

Without that stirring of air, it was sticky and sultry, but the ice cream cone was refreshingly cold. Trace strolled along the street in the general direction of the riverfront park atop the bluff and took his time eating the melting ice cream, licking it and letting its coldness glide down his throat.

There was already a small gathering of people in the park. Some were lounging on the grass and others were standing or tossing

Frisbees. The local school band was putting on a summer concert from the bandstand in the park. Brassy notes filled the air, sometimes discordant. A hot summer sun held its angle in the sky, stubbornly lingering above the horizon.

A scattering of lethargic applause followed the final note of a song. Trace stopped in the shade of an old oak on the edge of the park and rolled the ice cream around in his mouth. There was a break in the band's playing, a shuffling of music and licking of reeds. His glance wandered idly over the park grounds with their panoramic view of the bridge spanning the Mississippi River below and the green cluster of trees on the opposite bank.

His attention lingered on the stone marker, erected to commemorate the historic old trail known as the Natchez Trace. It had been established by the Indians long before any white men ever set foot on the continent, part of a trade route that extended as far north as the Great Lakes. In the settling of the nation it had been a post road for the mail, connecting Natchez to Nashville and creating a highway in the wilderness.

An announcement was being made from the bandstand and Trace let his gaze wander back to it. Only snatches of the words reached his hearing, the rest of it being carried away by the rushing breeze. He couldn't make heads or tails out of what was being said, but he recognized a couple of the local dignitaries on the bandstand. Some sort of plaque was being presented to a dark-haired woman in a cherry-red dress.

His tongue paused in its lick of the ice cream, the sight of Pilar momentarily jolting him. A restlessness ran through his nerve ends, coiling and uncoiling in frissons of tension. In the last two years he'd seen her, maybe, three times and the last one over seven months ago. Yet nothing had changed—not the feelings she aroused in him nor her stiffly cordial attitude toward him.

His gaze locked onto her form, searching for little details. She was wearing her hair shorter; its length brushed the tops of her shoulders now instead of cascading onto her back, and its style was fuller and softer. The material of her cherry-colored dress was a shiny fabric like silk, padded at the shoulders in an old-fashioned style with short capped sleeves. The soft wind caressed it, blowing it against her figure to outline the shape of her hips and thighs, then swirling it to hide them.

There was a movement in his side vision, and Trace glanced off his shoulder to see a stocky policeman ambling past him. More white hairs than iron gray were sticking out from under his cap. The short-sleeved shirt of his summer uniform was clinging damply to his thickening middle. Dark sunglasses protected his eyes, but it didn't keep Trace from recognizing him.

"Hey, Digger." It was a lazily drawled greeting that brought the man up short.

There was an initial blankness in Digger's

expression while Trace came under the scrutiny of those sunglasses before a surprised smile broke across Digger's face. He changed his course to wander over and stand next to Trace.

"Hell, I didn't know it was you standing there," he declared and rested his pudgy hands on his hips to let the air circulate around his body. "When did you make it back into town?"

"I grabbed a ride on the *Sophie B* when she left New Orleans." His attention strayed to the bandstand while he answered the question. "She dropped me under-the-hill about an hour ago."

"Are you gonna be in town for a spell? You've been comin' and goin' like a yo-yo lately. In and out, in and out. You've done more travelin' since you became a respectable businessman than you ever did before," Digger observed. "And here I thought you were gonna drop anchor."

"The whole system needed a major overhaul. It should start getting smoother." He munched on the sugar cone while he continued to watch the dark-haired woman on the bandstand.

"A lot of people didn't figure you'd stick it out. They thought you'd come into the business a-swingin' and a-fightin', then walk away when it was knee-deep in trouble."

"Weren't you one of them?" Trace slanted Digger a dryly amused glance and finished the ice cream cone. With a handkerchief from his pocket, he wiped the stickiness from his hands, momentarily draping his jacket over his arm, then swinging it over his shoulder again when he was done.

"Yeah," Digger admitted a little sheepishly.

Trace changed the subject. He'd already faced down all the doubts from others. Considering the heller he'd been, it wasn't surprising that no one believed he'd actually stay with it. There had been a couple of times when he'd wondered if it was worth the resistance he met on all fronts, including the men he'd worked with on the tugs.

"What's this all about?" He gestured to the bandstand, where Pilar was making some kind of acceptance speech. "Do you know?"

"It's some kind of civic award, recognizing all the things she's done for the betterment of the community or some such thing like that." Digger shrugged away the inexactness of his answer. "The idea of making it a public presentation was just a way of getting people to come to the concert."

At the conclusion of her short speech Trace joined in with the desultory applause, his jacket swinging from his mildly clapping hands. As she was escorted down the steps he hesitated, then glanced at Digger.

"Guess I might as well say hello to her so the gossips don't start talking about me being rude and ignoring my father's widow." It sounded like a good excuse.

"Yeah." A dry smile lifted the corners of the man's mouth as he seemed to gather up energy. "I'm supposed to be checkin' out a complaint about kids smokin' pot up here. Some poor old lady swears she could smell it. See ya later."

The band instructor lifted his baton and looked to see that all his young musicians were in readiness. The bronze plaque felt heavy in Pilar's arms, its wood sticking to her bare skin. She was hot and tired of smiling for everyone's benefit, but she was obliged to stay through a few more songs before it would be proper to leave.

At least she was out of that hot sun, and there was a breeze. She longed to take her shoes off and feel the cool grass under the bottoms of her feet. She feigned an attentiveness to the band's rendition of a popular song.

A hand lightly touched her arm, drawing her sharp glance to the auburn-haired woman standing with her. "Look who's here," Sandra Kay murmured, her eyes alive with interest as their glance went past Pilar. "I didn't know he was in town again, did you?"

When she saw Trace Santee strolling across the grass toward their small party, heat-raw nerves prickled. "Hardly." Her attention reverted to the bandstand in a struggling attempt at indifference.

"In a way it's a shame you and Trace never became close. After all, he is Elliot's son," Sandra Kay mused with absent regret, then shrugged faintly. "Of course, I don't think Trace has ever felt any strong family ties. He's always been something of a lone wolf." She lowered her voice even further, an indication to Pilar of Trace's imminent appearance. "I wish some psychiatrist would explain why women find rogues like Trace so attractive— even happily married women like myself. They always seem a little wicked, and a little dangerous. And I guess there's the feeling that if you had a wild little fling, he'd never tell."

It was just innocent female talk, but Pilar was agitated by it. She didn't care for the subject or Trace Santee. It had always been impossible to think of him as Elliot's son, especially since he was six years older than she was.

"Why, good evening, Trace." Sandra Kay greeted him, pretending that she hadn't seen him coming. "I never knew you attended something as tame as a band concert."

"On a lazy summer evening like this, who has the energy for anything more?" he countered with a sleepy look that was faintly sexy. When it wandered to Pilar, a thready tension caught her system in its web. "Evening, Pilar."

"Evening, Trace," she returned the greeting, a taut breathiness in her voice. All her senses were alert in a wary reaction to his presence while she maintained an attitude of aloofness.

The breeze had ruffled the virile thickness of his dark hair, and there was a bronze sheen to the chiseled angles and planes of his face.

His stance was relaxed, loose and at ease. The jacket of his summer-gray suit was slung over one shoulder, and the material of his shirt was sticking to his skin, outlining the flatly muscled chest and the width of his shoulders. The mat of chest hairs visible where his shirt was unbuttoned seemed to add to the reek of earthy masculinity. Pilar stiffened at its prepotency.

"I see you've thrown off your mourning rags." The idle roam of his gaze made her conscious of the way the breeze flattened the silk fabric of her dress against her figure. "New dress. New hairstyle. Very nice." The nod of approval seemed to dryly mock the changes.

"Thank you." There was a curling of her fingers into the palm of her hand, nails digging in to distract her sensitive nerves.

His glance drifted to the plaque she was holding. "I wasn't close enough to hear your speech after you were given the award. What's it for?"

He shifted to her side, angling his body to read the words engraved on the bronze shield as she tipped it away from her body.

There was no contact, but a rawness ran down her entire right side at the closeness. It was as if she could actually feel the heat of his body radiating onto her flesh, and the musky, warm smell of him was all around her. The agitated beat of her pulse only added to the brittle tension that wouldn't let her go.

"It's just a community service award." Pilar deliberately sounded off-hand about it, putting no special importance on the standardly worded plaque on which her name had been engraved.

"'In recognition of meritorious service—'" His voice trailed away after the beginning phrase as he skimmed the rest of the high-sounding words. Her sidelong glance checked to see if he had finished and met the taunting brilliance in his half-lidded eyes. "That should warm the cockles of your heart on a cold night."

"I have no doubt that something like this would mean nothing to you," she challenged, all smooth and poised on the outside, except for the glitter of anger in her eyes.

"I'm not likely to find out, since it's doubtful I'll ever be given one." Dryness riddled his voice, but there wasn't a hint of regret or remorse over the fact as Trace changed his position, creating more distance between them.

"That would be a day to mark on the calendar."

A suppressed laugh bubbled from Sandra Kay. Belatedly she and Pilar applauded the conclusion of a song by the band.

"How long are you going to be in Natchez this time?" Sandra Kay asked when they started playing again. "It seems like you're never here for more than a few days at a time."

"Everything seems to be running smoothly. So unless something comes up, I should be here for a while," he replied.

The confidence in his voice irritated Pilar. She didn't resist the urge to prick it. "The business may be running smoothly, but it still hasn't paid any dividends since you've taken over."

"No," Trace agreed, unaffected by her veiled barb. "But it's been operating inefficiently for some time. All the changes couldn't be accomplished overnight. But it's kept me busy and out of trouble." He gave her a considering look. "You've been busy, too. Everytime I pick up a local paper, I read Mrs. Santee this or Mrs. Santee attended that. No wonder they awarded you that plaque."

"I couldn't possibly keep up with her," Sandra Kay declared. "She's constantly going somewhere or doing something. It exhausts me just to look at her schedule. I don't see how she spends any time at Dragon Walk."

"Between the foundation and the antique business, I manage to keep busy, but it's hardly as grueling as you make it sound, Sandra Kay," Pilar insisted, but she did try to keep herself occupied as much as possible to avoid the loneliness of having nothing to do and no one to share idle time with.

"It sounds like 'all work and no play,'" Trace observed and appeared to study her closely, looking for signs of strain and overwork.

"'Idle hands are the devil's playground,'"

Pilar countered with another quotation and noticed his glance slide to her fingers.

"Lucky devil," he murmured in a very low voice, but the brief quirk of his mouth appeared harsh.

She chose to ignore the comment. "Regardless of Sandra Kay's opinion, I do have time to play. I just came back from spending two weeks with my parents in Virginia."

"It wasn't a vacation," Sandra Kay inserted in an aside to Trace. "She went antique buying."

The whole subject became distasteful to Pilar. "I don't think Trace is really interested in what I do with my time," she insisted to end this discussion and swung a cool glance at him. "There are a few boxes of things at Dragon Walk—family belongings like old photo albums, some of Elliot's personal items, and a few things that evidently belonged to your mother. When you have time, you can come by and pick them up."

"How about tonight?" he suggested. "It's Sunday, and I have nothing to do."

She was briefly thrown by his proposal, not expecting him to make it so soon. The boxes had been sitting in a corner of the old butler pantry for more than six months. She had postponed contacting him, knowing that sooner or later they were likely to see each other when he was in town, so there wasn't any need to make a special point of calling him.

"If that isn't convenient"—there was a faint

edge to his voice as his narrowed glance observed her reluctance—"I can come by another time. If you aren't home, I'm sure Cassie could show me where the boxes are."

"No," she heard herself say. "Tonight is fine. I wasn't planning to stay for the entire concert."

A flicker of surprise showed in his expression. "In that case, I'll stop out between eight thirty and nine."

"All right." She nodded stiffly in agreement.

"Do you see what I mean?" Sandra Kay spoke up. "She isn't satisfied doing just one thing tonight. Now she's arranged for you to come over and cart off a bunch of boxes."

The comment lifted the corners of his mouth slightly, but the movement carried only an acknowledgment of the words. "I'll see you later, then," he said, looking at Pilar.

There was a small inclination of her head. Her gaze watched him move away, leisurely strides carrying him out of the park. The rawness within her didn't go away.

When she pulled into the tree-lined driveway of Dragon Walk, a car turned in behind her. A glance in the rear-view mirror identified Trace as the driver. Her fingers flexed their grip on the steering wheel as she blanked out her thoughts and followed the lane that branched to the separate garage at the rear of the plantation house.

As Pilar walked out of the garage after putting the car away for the night, Trace was climbing out of his sedan. Nothing was said. Pilar was awkward with the silence, but she couldn't seem to break it. He was only a couple of steps behind her when she entered the house by the rear door.

"Cassie." Pilar was startled into speaking her name when she saw the black woman sitting at the kitchen table and looking very smart in a matching slack and summer-top set. "I thought you said you were going out this evening."

"I was and I am," she stated. "Eddie called twenty minutes ago to say he had a flat tire so he'd be late. He should be coming any time." A smile broke across her impatient expression when she saw Trace walk in behind Pilar. "When did you get back in town?"

"Late this afternoon. You've got a date tonight, have you?" he concluded with a twinkling look. "Eddie Tabor?"

"Yes, and no remarks from you are necessary," Cassie warned him, but the wideness of her smile took any strength from the response.

"I asked Trace to come by and pick up those boxes that are in the pantry." Pilar justified his presence and crossed to the serving alcove between the kitchen and the dining room to show him where they were.

"All of them?" he inquired, coming up behind her and glancing at the half-dozen boxes piled on top of each other in two stacks.

"Yes." She didn't pause in the small room for long, not liking the close quarters. "I've already been through them, so whatever you don't want to keep yourself, you can give away or dispose of however you want." She returned to the kitchen and walked straight to the refrigerator.

For an instant he let his gaze follow her, then swung his attention back to the boxes and walked over to size them up. From the kitchen came the rattle of ice cubes being dumped into a container. Trace hefted the top box and turned around to carry it outside to his car.

"Will you open the back door for me, Cassie?" When his request met with no response, he glanced at the black woman, who was looking worriedly after a departing Pilar. "Cassie?" The prompting of his voice attracted a blank stare.

"Did you want something? Oh, the door," she realized and moved to open it for him.

"Is something wrong?" Trace noticed the way her attention immediately returned to the inner door through which Pilar had disappeared.

"It's none of my business," Cassie insisted and the line of her mouth was pulled straight. "She's told me that often enough."

With the box in his arms, Trace had to wait until he had stowed it in the trunk of his car and returned to the kitchen before he could ask, "What is none of your business?" Cassie wouldn't have said that much if she didn't intend for him to know the rest of it.

"The way she's been drinking lately." She came straight to the point. "It started out so innocently . . . just a small drink before she went to bed to help her relax so she could sleep. Then it was a bigger one. Then it became two—sometimes three or more. Now she's at it again—loading up the ice bucket with cubes and carrying it off with her."

"Everybody has their own way of dealing with things." He made a deliberate attempt to sound indifferent, but there was a hardness in his features that hadn't been present before.

"I know what she's going through." Cassie sighed. "I went through it myself. It's something you fight at first 'cause you don't want to accept it. The loneliness eventually you can handle, but it's the hunger for a man that's tearing her up. Don't you look at me like that, Trace Santee," she reproved him sharply when he reared his head in open skepticism. "A woman has physical needs the same as a man. It doesn't make her bad to ache for the touch of a man's arms around her or the warmth of his body lying beside her in bed. That's a natural urge."

"I agree." Trace didn't argue with her point. "But, somehow, Pilar doesn't strike me as being quite as desperate as you're making her sound."

"Only because she's not ready to accept it," Cassie replied. "She drinks to pretend it's Elliot she's missing. She doesn't want to admit why she's hurting, because then she'd have to deal with the frustration of wanting, and having no one to satisfy that desire. She's going to have to face it sometime, just like everyone else who's lost their mate."

A car horn honked in the front driveway, signaling the arrival of Cassie's date and ending the conversation. Trace picked up a second box and carried it out the back door while he thought over the things Cassie had told him and tried to fit them with the image of self-sufficiency that Pilar projected.

Upstairs in her bedroom Pilar kicked off her low-heeled shoes and stripped out of her dress. It was too hot and sticky to put a lot of clothes back on, so she took a sleeveless wrap-around dress of strawberry-pink cotton from the large wardrobe closet and slipped it on, tying the sash into a bow at the side of her waist. She pushed the weight of her hair away from her face and secured it with a pair of combs. She heard the honking of a horn out front, followed by the shutting of the front door a few minutes later.

Before leaving the bedroom to go back downstairs, Pilar picked up the drink she'd set on the vanity and carried it with her. At the bottom of the stairs she hesitated, then walked to the kitchen. Trace was just heading out the back door with two of the lighter boxes in his arms.

"Are you managing all right?" she asked, conscious of the brief way his glance noted her change of attire.

"Yes." He pushed open the screen door with a corner of the boxes.

"Then I'll leave you to it," Pilar replied with a tense effort at indifference. "I'll be on the side porch if you should need help with anything."

On her way through the house she stopped in the den to collect the correspondence that needed answering as well as some auction circulars. There was still plenty of light on the west side of the house. Pilar spread her papers out on the glass top of a low wicker table that matched the rest of the white wicker furniture grouped around the porch in inviting clusters.

A breeze, cooled by the shade of the big oaks in the gardened front lawn, drifted onto the porch. Hanging baskets of pink and lavender fuchsia repeated the pastel colors of the patterned fabric covering the furniture cushions. Before Pilar took a seat on the narrow sofa, she went to the tall wicker stand where the ice bucket and bourbon decanter were placed. She added more cubes and a splash of bourbon to her watery drink.

Sitting down, she picked up the auction circulars first and began to check their dates with her appointment calendar. She leaned forward and absently rubbed the cool, moist glass against her cheek. She tried not to listen to the sounds of the back door slamming as Trace made his trips to the car with the boxes.

When the last one was sitting in the rear seat of his car, Trace pulled a handkerchief from his hip pocket and wiped at the perspiration trickling down his neck. On a sultry evening like this it didn't take much effort to work up a sweat. He rubbed the kerchief over the top of his lip and glanced absently toward the porch. With a slow gathering of his muscles, Trace turned and walked in that direction.

At the side steps leading up to the porch he paused. His glance was pulled to the figure of Pilar, seated on the white-backed cushions with sprays of pink flowers. She was leaning forward, studying some papers on a wicker table. Her legs were crossed, the skirt of her dress splitting to provide him with a view of a creamy thigh. There was a stirring pressure in his loins. With a tightened jaw, Trace climbed the steps to the porch. Her glance skipped to him, then back to the papers where it stayed as she took a swallow from the glass she was holding.

"Didn't anybody ever tell you you shouldn't drink alone?" Trace remarked dryly and walked to the stand to help himself to the bourbon and ice.

"At the end of a day I find a drink pleasantly relaxing," she returned smoothly, barely looking up when he wandered over to the wicker chair with the tall, fan-shaped back.

"Just one drink?" He glanced pointedly at the quantity of liquor in her squat glass, which couldn't all be attributed to melting ice cubes.

"Sometimes a large one," Pilar admitted with a challenging tilt of her head. After that earlier rawness in his presence, she felt pleasantly loose and able to deal with him. It showed in the artificially bold glint in her dark eyes.

Her shoulders were hunched to allow her forearms to rest on her crossed legs. The action allowed the crossing front of her wraparound dress to gape slightly. Trace's angle from the chair permitted him to view the exposed slope of a breast. There was a hardness in the steel-gray of his eyes as he tried not to look, but his gaze kept slipping to it. Pilar appeared totally oblivious to the exposure—and to him.

"Were you able to load all the boxes in your car?" she asked while she ran a pencil down a list of items on a paper.

"Yes, I did."

Outside of a nod, she didn't appear interested in his answer as she flipped pages in an appointment calendar, then thoughtfully rubbed the soft eraser end of the pencil along her lower lip. Its slow movement was an unwanted diversion that had his mouth pressed tightly shut.

Everything about her—from the way she sat to the way she was dressed to her gestures—seemed to be deliberately provocative, designed to arouse and stimulate. Yet she showed about as much interest in him as she did a piece of furniture. They were conflicting signals, her body flashing him one set, and her attitude slapping him away.

If he thought for one minute that she knew what she was doing to him, he'd . . . Trace cut off the thought because there was no answer to it. He had to move out of that chair while he still had a grip on himself.

Chapter Six

*R*ising, Trace took a quick swig of his drink and walked to the tall wicker table to replenish it. Silently he blamed Cassie and her talk for all his wild imaginings. For purely selfish reasons he wanted to believe that Pilar was attempting to be alluring for him.

When he finally turned back to face her, she had shifted her hands to the seat cushion and stiffened her arms in a bracing posture that emphasized the jutting roundness of her breasts. Yet she continued to look at the papers on the table with thoughtful concentration.

"What's so interesting?" A hint of gruffness put an edge on his question.

"What?" Her dark glance hardly touched

him, but she did shift out of that pose to a less disturbing one. "I'm trying to decide how I could rearrange my schedule so I could attend this auction. They have a silver service by Reed and Barton listed that I'd like to see, as well as some Meissen porcelain."

"Where is it?" Trace wandered over to look at the flyer.

"Just outside of Vicksburg." She scratched out the appointment listed on the day of the sale, changed it to another date, and wrote in the auction. Something was marked on nearly every day, and Trace noticed, when she had turned pages, that many of them were auctions.

"You go to a lot of them, don't you?" He swirled the liquid in his glass to hasten the cooling by the ice cubes.

"Yes. They're fun, especially those rare times when you find some treasure that the people didn't even know they had. And there's always that competitive edge when you're bidding against another dealer on some piece you'd kill for," Pilar declared with a faint laugh that derided the seriousness of her statement. Her head was tilted back to look up at him, her features all womanly soft and impishly gay.

"All you'd have to do is bat those long, black lashes at him and he'd forget all about the item on the auction block," Trace informed her in a thickening voice and took a fiery swallow of his drink to burn out the fire that had suddenly blazed.

"The problem is when it's another woman," she retorted and took a sip of her drink. "It needs freshening," she murmured and glided to her feet in a graceful motion.

Her path to the table brought her close to him, close enough for the fragrance of her hair to stir up his senses. But as she passed he noticed that she was weaving slightly.

"Maybe it's time I was leaving," he muttered, too aware that there was no one else around.

"You haven't finished your drink." She gave him a short look of surprise. "After loading all those boxes in the car, you might as well take a few minutes to cool off." She turned her back to him again, and he heard the clink of ice being dropped into a glass.

Needing a diversion, he picked up her appointment calendar and flipped through a few pages. "You're going to be in New Orleans the middle of July?"

"Yes." She turned to see the appointment book in his hand but made no sign that she objected. "I try to go there a couple of times a year just to browse through some of the smaller antique shops in the suburbs. Sometimes it's an easy way to find a bargain or to locate the fourth chair to some table set of a client."

"That's about the time a new towboat is supposed to be coming out of the shipyards. Maybe if the dates coincide, you can come to her launching."

"Maybe." She didn't dismiss the suggestion, but she didn't appear interested in it either.

Masking his frustration, Trace studied the datebook again. "I don't see many social engagements listed."

"Couples are usually invited to parties," she informed him smoothly and crossed the wooden deck to remove the leather-bound appointment book from his hand. "Single women tend to be the bane of most social gatherings. Half the wives are afraid that I am so sexually deprived that I'll seduce their husbands if I'm alone with them for more than five minutes. And half the husbands are hoping that I will." There was a bitter ring of ironic amusement in her voice.

"You could always arrange to have a male escort," Trace countered. "I don't believe that you haven't had volunteers."

"In case you haven't noticed, there isn't exactly a surfeit of single males over the age of thirty in this area. When you find one, I can almost guarantee there'll be something wrong with him. If he isn't grotesquely overweight, stupid, or a drunkard, then he's probably an ex-wife beater. Besides, I'm not that desperate for a man," she declared coolly.

"Aren't you?"

Pilar didn't like the way he looked at her when he said that. There was something dry and measuring about it that set off little twinges of unease. He reached out and lightly rubbed the back of his knuckles down the bareness of her arm. The unexpected caress of his hand stunned her, and she pulled away from it. The sudden action made her a little dizzy.

"No, I'm not," she retorted.

"You want to be looked at, but you don't want to be touched . . . by anyone. Is that it?" he murmured.

"I don't know what you're talking about." Her pulse fluctuated wildly as she avoided his eyes, stiff and resistant to their probe.

"I'm not sure that I do, either." There was the clunk of a glass being set down. Then a hand, cool from the iced glass, was gripping her arm, its pressure firm but not forceful. Pilar let herself be turned to face him squarely. Defiance ran hotly through her blood. "Maybe you can explain some things to me."

"If you don't know what you're talking about, it isn't likely I will," she countered with frosty indifference, but she felt unsteady.

"What am I doing here tonight?" he challenged.

"What a ridiculous question!" Pilar declared with incredulous amusement. "You came to collect things that belonged to your family." She swung away from him and started to take a sip of the bourbon, but Trace took the glass from her hand before it touched her mouth.

"You've had enough to drink," he stated and ignored the indignant breath she drew in protest of his high-handed action. This time he held both her arms so she couldn't turn away. "Now, tell me—why tonight?"

"It was your idea," she reminded him curtly. "I didn't suggest it."

"But you agreed to it," Trace countered, watching her closely. "And you agreed to it believing that Cassie wasn't home—that she would be out for the evening."

"So? That has no bearing on it. I'm not afraid to be alone with you," she insisted and raked him with a look designed to put him in his place.

"And I can't believe you're usually this careless about the way you dress. A couple of times I had the impression I was watching the beginning act of some striptease show with all the leg and breast you kept showing me."

"What?!" She pulled back in shock, her hands pushing at his chest while heat fanned her cheeks. "I didn't wear this dress for your prurient pleasure. It's cool and comfortable."

"I'm sure it is, especially when all you're wearing under it is a pair of panties. Or are you going to tell me that I wasn't supposed to notice that either?" His hands shifted, gripping her waist while her straining arms maintained a wedge between them.

"You're disgusting." She was so angry she couldn't think.

"It makes it easier, doesn't it?" The gleam in his gray eyes hardened. "Easier than looking at the facts. You told me to come, knowing you'd be here alone. The first thing you did was to slip into 'something more comfortable.'" He put suggestive emphasis on the phrase. "Then you had a few drinks before I joined you so you could pretend you didn't know what you were doing."

"That's a lie. You're just twisting things," Pilar accused angrily but her head was swimming.

"Maybe I am. And maybe this is all a calculated move on your part," he challenged harshly. "I would have left ten minutes ago but you wanted me to stay. You were the one who introduced the subject of sex and made all the comments about sexual deprivation— not me. You were choreographing a dance, but I threw you out of step, didn't I, when I didn't wait for you to provoke me into making a pass."

It all sounded so damning that she was hot all over. It was impossible to look at him. She felt weak and sick. When his hands slid onto her spine, she didn't resist the molding pressure that brought her into contact with the lower half of his body.

"How can you say that?" she protested.

"Because it's true." His voice turned husky. When she looked up, there was a smoldering darkness in his eyes. The porch seemed to spin crazily for a minute, and Pilar wondered how much she had drunk.

"You probably didn't consciously plan all of it. Instinct did a lot of it," he said. "The instinct that wanted to feel a man's arms around you again—the need to have physical contact with another human being. And you picked me because you knew I had succumbed to the temptation of you once before."

"No!" Pilar was insistent. "It's all a mistake."

"Is it? Then why aren't you fighting me?" he demanded.

And she realized how passive she was in his arms, offering him no more than token resistance. She suddenly began to wonder if everything he'd said was true. Had she subconsciously wanted this? Her stunned and widened gaze searched the hard, male features that were only inches from her own. She stared at his mouth.

There was a tentative movement toward it, as if she had to discover whether she wanted to feel the sensation of it on her lips. A hand moved up her spine, applying pressure to bring her closer.

When her dazed senses alerted her to the downward descent of his mouth, Pilar stiffened. By then it seemed to be too late. There was an instant of strangeness and uncertainty, an absence of familiarity in the pervasive kiss. But its heat was addictive and Pilar let it consume her, reeling under the waves of warm sensation. She was so empty inside, so raw with wanting that nothing else seemed to matter—not who was holding her, or why.

Her lips were ravished, eaten whole, while her body was warmed and made to live again by the heated male flesh of his long, muscled form. The crush of his hands alternately explored and caressed the shape of her shoulders and the sensitive curve of her spine, pressing and arching until there was contact from head to toe.

The more she strained against him, the more she seemed to receive. Her fingers spread across the bunching muscles along the back of his shoulders, living steel that moved under her touch. The sawing, driving pressure of his mouth separated her lips and swallowed the faint moan that came from her throat. She was plunged into an abyss of mindless lust, all swirling heat and raging fire.

Nothing existed but the heady taste of him filling her mouth and the musky, stimulating male odor clinging to his skin. She was drunk with sensation and longing for more. She couldn't seem to absorb enough of him into her to ease all the places that ached.

His fingers snarled into her hair as he moistly dragged his kiss across cheek and jaw to an ear. Pilar shuddered uncontrollably at the rush of his warm breath into the sensitive area that set off a whole chain of excited vibrations. She could hardly breathe herself; it was so heavy and labored, disturbed to the point that the blood was pounding through her veins.

"This is what you wanted, isn't it?" The male voice was husky and rough, demanding an admission while that burning mouth continued to wreak havoc over her skin.

It was trying to drag her back into reality. Pilar didn't want that. There was a faint movement of her head in protest, and an absently impatient frown touched her brow. "Don't talk," she whispered with aching insistence. "Don't say anything."

Her fingers made a tactile journey to the lean angle of his jaw and tried to lift it and turn it so her lips could find their male counterpart and occupy them with more intimate communication. But she met with resistance, then withdrawal as his head was pulled back. Her eyelids were heavy, but she dragged them open, unable to look higher than the tantalizing outline of his mouth.

"Look at me." It was an insistent order, pitched low with a graveled edge.

A hand was on her face, managing to touch and stroke with a kind of unwillingness while it lifted her chin to elevate her gaze. There was so much blackness in his eyes that the gray color was a mere silver ring. Behind the hardness of their study, desire smoldered hotly.

"Isn't this what you wanted when you told me to come here tonight?" he demanded again. "Admit it, Pilar. You wanted this to happen."

"No." She had to reject that any of this was premeditated. It was too damning to do otherwise.

A host of perceptions hit her at once from the abandoned way she was straining into the hard contact with his hips, to the way she was arching to flatten her breasts against the muscled solidness of his chest. The embrace was all so intimate, a prelude to mating. And that face, ruggedly lean and hollowed, staring down into hers knew exactly what it signified.

"No!" Her second denial rushed on the heels of the first, more strident.

With a little push she was out of his arms, but they had made no attempt to hold her. Pilar didn't stop as she ran to the glassed doors that led into the parlor, briefly feeling the rush of a cool wind over her hot skin. Then she was inside and shutting the doors to back away from them a few steps before turning into the room. But she wasn't able to shut the inner doors on all the rawness and fierce ache coming from her body.

There was the metal click of a door latch, and Pilar whirled toward the sound. When Trace stepped into the room, a dark shape against the waning outside light, her heart catapulted into her throat. No attempt was made to cross the room as he faced her, his tall body tapering leanly from wide shoulders to narrow hips.

"I was supposed to follow you in here, wasn't I?" There was a harsh ring to his low voice.

Her lips parted on a quickly indrawn breath, but she couldn't find the words to deny his charge. There was a terrible ringing in her head that hammered her with the truth. Sexual desire and passion were feelings she had forced into dormancy, refusing to air them or acknowledge them. Only the dead couldn't feel the desire for bodily contact, and she wasn't dead. She'd simply bottled her needs inside until they reached the flashpoint tonight when she'd been presented with an opportunity to satisfy them. On some animal level of her subconscious, she had maneuvered Trace, herself, everything.

"Yes." The admission came out with a broken little cry as Pilar averted her face, still inwardly reeling from the discovery about herself.

"You knew you could count on me to come through, didn't you?" His tone remained harshly cynical and slowly came closer. "After all, I'm completely unscrupulous— without any morals. If you tried this with anyone else, there was always the risk they might be slow on the uptake and not recognize the subtle signals you were flashing. It could have forced you to be blatant. This way you can always allow yourself the excuse that you'd been drinking more than you realized and Trace Santee, the corrupt bastard that he is, took advantage of you in a vulnerable moment."

"Stop it." Pilar clenched her hands into fists and pressed them to her ears, trying to block out the burrowing words that stripped her bare.

His circling fingers caught her wrists and pulled them down. Her arms remained rigidly bent, straining in mute protest of his action.

Haunted by the way she had tried to use him so she wouldn't have to feel any guilt or remorse, her dark eyes tentatively lifted their glance to his face.

There was a relentless quality to the chiseled bones in it, a lack of expression that seemed to make her heart beat faster. His hooded eyes never wavered from their inspection of her. In the shadows of the house interior, his hair seemed almost devil-black.

"You wanted to be made love to and you picked me. Didn't you?" Again he sought her confirmation.

"Yes." Almost impatiently she pushed it out with a hissing breath.

His fingers loosened their hold on her wrists, and there seemed no place for her hands to go except onto the front of his shirt. His own hands glided to the sides of her back, the warmth of them flowing across her ribs. The vein in her throat began to throb heavily.

"Pilar." The low, raw urging expressed a reluctant want that she understood.

It broke through her restraint. "Yes." Her hands went around his corded neck and pressed at the back of his head to bring his mouth down onto hers.

His arms gathered her inside their circle while his lips rolled onto hers in a fevered rush of moisture and heat. Pilar dug her fingers into the springing thickness of his hair to increase the crushing pressure of his driving kiss. She couldn't breathe, but it didn't matter. Her body strained to mold itself to the hard male contours, her flesh absorbing their exciting imprint.

There was a wild and hungry mating of lips and tongues, a restlessness in the press of bodies that couldn't get close enough. It was the intimacy of a man and a woman that Pilar needed. There was a feminine fierceness about the way she responded to him, her lips traveling over a smoothly shaven cheek and jaw and tasting the salty perspiration that beaded on his upper lip.

Her breath came in quick, hot rushes as she nibbled at the corded muscle standing out so tautly in his neck. Her fingers tugged at the buttons of his shirt. A little thrill shot through when she heard the half-muffled groan that shuddered him as her fingers crept inside his shirt and onto his bare flesh. Her hands sensually explored his chest and the virile mat of curly hair scattered across sinewed breastbones.

Something pulled at the waistline of her wraparound dress and its tightness suddenly loosened when the bow securing it was untied. The front of the strawberry-pink dress was pushed open, and Pilar breathed in sharply at the stabbing pleasure that quivered through her when the rough texture of a man's hand glided onto her naked skin. The devastation wrought on her senses by his cupping hands was virtually total.

Her lungs welled with air and expanded her

rib cage to push her breasts more fully into his stimulating hands while his thumbs rubbed and teased her nipples into hard, erect nubs. She felt tensely weak, all heady and taut with wanting more, but lacking the strength to do more than savor the raw sensations. His mouth came back to devour her lips in a kiss that seemed to rock her all the way to her toes.

Impatient hands pushed the sleeveless dress off her shoulders and Pilar lowered her arms to let it slide to the floor, glad to be rid of the hampering garment. His shirt was already pulled loose from the waistband of his pants. When she came against him again, she knew the searing intoxication of flesh touching flesh.

There was a movement, a turning, a step when he took all of her weight. Then she was being lowered, and there were cushions beneath her and the force of his body bearing down. His mouth was all over her, nibbling at her neck and nipping at her shoulders until her skin danced with raw quivers, then shifting to nuzzle at her breasts and erotically suckle at them until the ache in the pit of her stomach seemed unbearable.

But his hands seemed to know that, caressing and massaging with wicked deftness. Pilar writhed and twisted, half crazy with the sweet torment of his touch. Her fingernails dug into the muscled flesh of his back, urgent in their attempt to force the hard weight of him onto her.

There was a moment of withdrawal when he pulled away from her. A tortured sound of protest came from her throat at the cessation of all contact with him.

It took a second for her passion-thick senses to locate him. He was standing alongside the sofa where she lay, his hands at the buttoned closing of his trousers while he stared down at her. There was something in his eyes that she didn't understand—almost indecision.

Her hungry glance skimmed the dark hairs on his bronze chest, traveling down his flatly muscled stomach. "Trace," she urged him in a voice that throbbed on an aching note.

A **muscle** leaped convulsively along his jaw, and he swung away from the sofa, one step striding into another. Stunned, Pilar turned onto her side and watched as he began to shove his shirttail inside his pants.

"Trace." This time it was confusion and bewildered questioning that dominated her thready voice.

Her dress was scooped off the floor and tossed sideways to her, landing softly on her shoulder and sliding down before Pilar could react and catch it. Unconsciously she clutched it in front of her, compelled by some unbidden instinct to cover her nakedness even though Trace wasn't looking at her. His dark head was bent as he buttoned his shirt with jerky impatience, his body angled away from her.

"You aren't leaving now?" The shameless protest was wrenched from her by all the strident needs he'd aroused, then failed to satisfy.

His head half-turned in her direction, giving her a glimpse of his profile and all the tautly checked emotions that gave it a hard look. "I guess you'll just have to face the fact that I can't be the animal you'd like me to be." The tersely worded statement was pushed through clenched teeth.

"No." She choked on the muffled cry as Trace headed for the porch doors, his stride lengthening.

Only seconds later, it seemed, his car roared out of the driveway. Pilar sat huddled on the sofa with the cotton dress clutched to her, twice as empty and hurting twice as much. Sickened and ashamed, she was caught halfway between frustration and pain as hot tears rolled down her lashes.

The knot of his tie was loosened and the top button of his shirt was unfastened. Trace conformed to the practice of wearing a business suit and tie to the office in the morning, but the jacket usually came off when he walked in the door. After lunch the tie was loosened. If it was late in the day, the tie was off and the cuffs of his shirt were turned back.

A small staff meeting was in progress, but it wasn't going well. Trace was at the core of the crackling in the air, his ill temper managing to make all three department heads uncomfortable in his presence, never sure which of them would bear the brunt of it next. In other

years that bad mood would have been un-
leashed in some physical form, but trapped in
an office, it had no outlet.

"What the hell do you mean, Connors, that
you couldn't finish your report because you
didn't get all the numbers back from our
accounting firm?" Trace pushed out of his
chair, despising this endless paperwork yet
aware that it was a necessary evil. "Weren't
they supposed to have that information for
you last week?"

"Yes, but Tom . . . Mr. Lowe . . . got sick
and—" The man attempted an explanation.

"I don't give a damn who got sick!" Trace
flared. "That firm is being paid to do a job for
us. It isn't *our* problem how they accomplish
it! And if they are so understaffed they can't
do it, maybe it's time we changed accoun-
tants."

"I don't think that's necessary." A flustered
Connors protested the rashness of that statement.

"You don't," Trace challenged grimly and
walked to the water pitcher on the credenza to
fill a glass with ice water. "I didn't have to
make the trip up from New Orleans. There
were some loose ends I could have cleared up
if I had stayed a couple more days instead of
arranging to return here to Natchez last night
—so we could hold this meeting. And it's only
half a meeting because you don't have your
report ready."

The thing that kept tearing at him was the
knowledge that if he'd stayed in New Orleans

that extra day, he would have spared himself
last night's agony. It damn near ripped him
apart. Trace bolted down a swallow of ice
water like he was downing a shot of whiskey.
The cold, bracing liquid seemed to have a
similar effect, its iciness shocking his throat.

"I know I'll have the report ready for you by
Wednesday, Trace," Connors offered hesitantly.

"Wednesday." Trace pivoted, still too irritated and on edge to be mollified by that
promise.

A knock preceded the opening of the door to
his private office. The peremptory intrusion
was another irritant to an already growing
list. Trace threw a cold look at the middle-
aged woman opening his door.

"What the hell is it now, Maude? I told
you—" The sight of Pilar standing in the background behind his secretary cut off the rest of
the complaint he was about to make.

"Mrs. Santee is here. I thought you'd want
to see her." There was an imperious lift of
Maude Hanks' dye-darkened head. She had
ruled the office for too many years to bow to
any higher authority. And in her book protocol
dictated that an owner of the company be
admitted at any time, regardless of the inter-
ruption of normal schedules.

"If I'm interrupting a meeting, I can come
back later," Pilar suggested at Trace's long
hesitation.

A pair of glasses, half shaded with a smoky-
blue color on the top of the lenses, obscured

the darkness of her eyes. He could see them, yet he couldn't read their expression. Her shiny onyx hair was loosely swept back from her face and coiled in a chic bun, not flowing freely as it had been when she had lain on the couch, all creamy white skin and silky black hair, for the feasting of his hungry eyes. And this dress was a gauzy thing in a deep shade of turquoise blue that covered her from neck to wrists, a dark underslip hiding the ripe and full breasts that had been his to fondle and kiss.

"No. Come in," he said abruptly and rudely turned away from the door before other vivid details came back to him. "We were just finishing up." The nod of his head was curt and dismissive to the three men. "You can leave now."

"Thank you, Maude," Pilar murmured to the woman who had been her husband's secretary and passed by her into the office.

She nodded briefly to the men filing past her to leave, all the while conscious of Trace as he donned the mustard-colored blazer that had been hooked over the corner of a chair and adjusted the tie. Her legs felt weak, and she still wasn't sure she had the courage to go through with this.

He seemed so distant, hard and uncaring. When he walked behind the desk, putting it between them, she didn't think he could have been further away from her.

"What is it you wanted to see me about?" He

took a cigarette from the pack on his desk and lit it, not looking at her as he asked the question.

The door was shut behind her, the sound briefly distracting her. When she glanced back, Trace was still standing behind the desk, the smoke from the cigarette throwing up a screen.

"I came"—she took a step toward his desk and unsnapped her clutch purse to remove a small, narrow packet—"because I'm out selling tickets for a charity dinner to raise money for—" The falseness of her claim rang blatantly in her ears, and Pilar didn't finish the lie. "That's not why I'm here," she admitted and stared at the charity tickets that were her excuse.

"Oh?" It was an almost disinterested challenge.

"I came to thank you for not—" Somehow she couldn't put it into words when she looked at him. All the heat and embarrassment came rushing back.

His mouth quirked at a mocking angle. "For not allowing myself to be seduced by my father's wife?" Trace suggested.

"Yes." Pilar bent her head, breathing tightly. "I wanted you to know that I'm grateful you stopped when you did. It was very—"

"Noble?" Trace interrupted to suggest a descriptive adjective.

"Yes, noble," she agreed, a little wary as she eyed him again.

"It wasn't a damned bit noble," he declared,

making a scoffing sound in his throat. Trace walked from behind the desk to sit sideways on the edge of it. "It was purely selfish."

"Selfish," Pilar murmured, confused by his answer.

"In the morning I knew you'd hate yourself —but not nearly as much as you'd hate me," Trace explained calmly while he continued to watch her. "Once I would have taken what you offered and let the devil handle tomorrow."

"I'm glad you didn't." She breathed a little easier. "Because you're right. I would have hated myself this morning. And I doubt if I could have faced you. As it is, I feel like a fool."

"It's forgotten." He half turned away from her to flick the ash from his cigarette into a ceramic ashtray on his desktop. "We all get lonely at times and need to be loved. Sometimes we aren't careful about whom we choose. It's part of what makes the world go around."

"I . . . don't know what to say." She was hesitant, wondering more than a little if he wasn't making a personal observation about himself.

"Tell me how much those tickets are for that charity dinner," he suggested with a dry gleam.

"You don't have to buy any." Pilar shook her head, aware that he was merely turning the conversation away from an unpleasant subject.

"I might as well." He reached into the side pocket of his suit pants and removed some folded bills, peeling off two of the larger bills. "Since I seem to be turning respectable, I might as well go all the way." When she reluctantly started to separate several tickets from the packet, he shook his head. "Just give me one ticket. You can consider the rest a donation."

"You're being too generous, Trace." Her voice was pitched low. Pilar almost preferred that he'd say some of the cutting observations he'd made the night before rather than act like nothing very important had happened. "It's mainly a social gathering."

"Are you going?" After they had exchanged the ticket and the money, he slipped the numbered ticket into the inside breast pocket of his jacket.

"I'll put in an appearance. It's expected." That came with the position she'd carved for herself in the community.

"It might be a good place for you to find yourself a boyfriend," Trace stated and straightened from the desk. The action hinted that he had work to do if she was finished.

"Yes, it might." Somehow she wasn't looking forward to all the uncertainty and awkwardness that came with dating. She slipped the money and the rest of her tickets inside

her purse and clicked it shut. "Good-bye,
Trace."

"Good-bye." He walked her to the door, giving her the distinct feeling that it was merely
a show of formal courtesy. When she walked
out of the office, Pilar felt that somehow she'd
been let down.

Chapter Seven

$\mathcal{T}$he skirt of her violet-flowered chiffon dress floated softly against her legs as Pilar descended the staircase at Dragon Walk. The metallic clapping of the ornate brass knocker on the front door seemed to echo through the big house. Pilar hurried across the cypress floors in a running walk, her pale lavender heels clicking swiftly across the waxed boards.

There was a faint impatience in her expression for the unknown caller. This afternoon she had allowed herself to be persuaded to take tickets at the charity dinner that night, so she needed to be there early. She was already running late.

When she opened the heavy front door, she

was prepared to deal quickly with whoever it was and send them on their way. But she hadn't anticipated that Trace would be standing outside. Her startled glance ran over the dark suit and tie he was wearing and the damp sheen of his thick black hair.

His mouth quirked in an engaging half-smile. "Hello."

"Hello." She couldn't keep that note of surprise out of her voice and gripped the edge of the open door to conceal the little burst of agitation.

"I have this ticket for dinner tonight, but I've never been too keen about attending affairs like this. You mentioned once that you weren't exactly welcome without an escort. I thought I'd offer my services tonight."

"I . . ." Her hesitation was brief as she came to a quick decision. "All right. Only I have to leave now. I've volunteered to take tickets."

"My car's parked right out front."

She bit at the inside of her lip, belatedly wondering if she hadn't acted impulsively, but she wasn't going to back out now. "Just give me a minute to get my purse and lock the back door."

It took her less time than that. Trace waited on the porch while she locked the front door, then walked with him to the car parked in the circle drive. Before shutting the door, he lifted the skirt of her dress out of the way.

"Where's Cassie?" Trace asked when he slipped behind the wheel. "Isn't she home?"

"No. She's at the Thorsons' tonight. Old Mr. Thorson is in bed with a severe case of influenza, and Mrs. Thorson suffers from chronic asthma. She can barely take care of herself, let alone look after him. So Cassie went over to take care of both of them."

"Thorson." Trace repeated the name thoughtfully. "I remember him. I used to steal watermelons out of his patch all the time." He darted her a twinkling look that was wicked with devilment. "I don't think he ever knew that I'd found out he loaded his shotgun with watermelon seeds. Every time he fired off that sawed-off cannon of his, I used to laugh. Which just made him madder." There was a faint shake of his head, a smile of warm recollection in his expression. "Those were the sweetest watermelons I ever tasted."

"It's a wonder Cassie doesn't have more gray hairs than she has," Pilar murmured, shuddering to think what a hellion he must have been as a boy, always prime for trouble.

"Why do you say Cassie instead of Elliot?" His glance strayed from the traffic on the road long enough to wander curiously over her profile.

"I don't know. I suppose because . . . women worry about such things more than men." She shrugged, then probed with a question of her own. "Why were you such a rebel?"

"Now you're making it sound as if I've suddenly reformed," Trace mocked.

"Not totally," Pilar replied after thinking

about the answer for a few seconds. "I think
you still like to fly in the face of convention.
Sometimes I think you took over the barge
line just to shock everyone."

"That was probably part of it," he conceded
idly. "Why did you stay in Natchez after Elliot
died? You have no ties here. All your family is
back in Virginia."

"I thought about it," she admitted while she
glanced out the window at the lush greenery
of trees gilded with silvery Spanish moss.
Natchez was a treasure house of antebellum
homes, with nearly a hundred still standing.
"But I loved the area. And my antique shop
was doing well, and I had managed to estab-
lish a clientele of repeat customers. If I left,
I'd have to start all over again. What was the
point?"

There was already a scarcity of parking
spaces when they arrived on the grounds of
one of the more imposing plantation homes
located in Natchez. Sandra Kay Austin
snared them as they entered the house.

"It's about time you arrived," she mildly
chided Pilar for her tardiness. "Loretta is
filling in for you. I see you managed to per-
suade Trace to come with you. It's about time
we put this man into circulation." Her eyes
flirted with him, feeling safely bold because of
the wedding ring on her finger. "Now, you
stay clear of all those pretty young things,
Trace Santee, or some daddy is liable to tear
you apart. This is supposed to be a party."

"I'll do my best to remember that, Sandra Kay," he promised lazily.

"I have half a notion not to let you out of my sight just to see that you do," the auburn-haired woman playfully warned him. "They've set up a little bar in the south parlor for you men so you can enjoy a drink before they begin serving from the buffet."

"In that case, I might as well head in that direction," Trace said and glanced at Pilar. "Would you like me to bring you a drink from the bar? Taking tickets might be thirsty business."

"No, thank you." Her glance dropped swiftly from his. It was too fresh in her memory—the way she'd tried to pretend that alcohol had lowered her resistance to his sexual advances. "If I make any mistakes tonight, I don't want to try to blame it on drinking."

"No drinking on the job has always been a sound policy," came the bland agreement, but Pilar knew he'd caught her reference. "I'll let you get to work."

As he walked down the great hall that divided the house down the middle, Sandra Kay sighed and shook her head. "It's a downright sin for a man to be so wickedly handsome. Given half a chance, I swear he'd be out dueling under the oaks before the night's out, like they did in the old days." The front door opened to admit more arriving guests. "You'd better go relieve Loretta before those daggers she's throwing at me become real ones."

The turnout for the dinner was large, filling the double parlor rooms with people and spilling them into the wide, long hallway. Dinner was served from two giant buffet tables. Unable to leave her post at the door, Pilar insisted that Trace go through the line and not wait for her.

When she was finally relieved, she wasn't able to find him in the confusion of people. The Silvertons invited her to join them at their table, along with several out-of-town guests they were entertaining. The conversation at the table was lively and interesting. It wasn't long before Pilar stopped looking for Trace and began to enjoy the company of her dinner companions.

The man sitting beside her had a ready laugh to go along with his strong and smiling face. His hair was the color of a dark copper penny, burnished and gleaming under the globed light of a massive chandelier. Pilar hadn't caught his last name when they were introduced, but his first name was Ben. And she was aware of the interest in his eyes when he looked at her.

"Pilar. That's a Spanish name, isn't it?" he asked, drawing her into a private conversation while they lingered at the table over coffee.

"Yes. My mother liked it." Pilar shrugged, since her naming had no special significance beyond that.

"Was that your brother I met earlier tonight? I'm sure his name was Santee. Tall, with black hair just like yours and a small scar on his cheek." He described him for her.

"You must mean Trace." The description fit no one else. Unconsciously she let her glance make an idle search of the dinner guests still gathered in the room, some at tables and some standing in small groups.

"Yeah, that was his name. I remembered it was an unusual one, just like yours." He nodded. "Are you two related?"

"Only by marriage." She noticed the bus-boys hovering close by. "I think they'd like to clear the tables now that we're all finished eating," she said to prompt those at her table into leaving.

"Is there a drawing room where we can repair to?" another of the Silvertons' guests inquired, mockingly adopting an old-fashioned phraseology.

"I believe the bar has opened." Frank Silverton pushed his chair away from the table and stood to assist his wife.

"You'll be joining us, won't you?" Ben inquired as he courteously helped Pilar to her feet.

"I think I should look for my escort. I was busy at the door taking tickets so Trace went through the buffet line earlier," she explained with casual ease.

"Trace brought you?" Maryann Silverton looked at her with vague surprise. "How nice that you didn't have to come alone."

"Well, knowing Trace," her husband inserted, "he's probably at the bar, so you might as well walk with us."

But he wasn't in the south parlor, where most of the dinner guests had gathered to socialize. Pilar wandered among the scattered clusters, stopping to chat with this person and that acquaintance. Someone had always "just seen Trace" in the next room or talking to so-and-so in the hall. But she continually missed catching up with him. Finally she ended up in the south parlor where she started. The attractively handsome, copper-haired Ben was quickly at her side to urge her to rejoin their group.

"Couldn't you find him?" Frank Silverton's smile didn't show much surprise, as if Trace's disappearance was expected.

"I've lost him somewhere," Pilar admitted. "I decided I might as well stay in one place and let him find me when he's ready to leave."

"We were just going outside onto the veranda for some fresh air," Maryann stated. "Hopefully it won't be so noisy and crowded out there."

The languid night air was scented with the fragrance of roses climbing and twisting on the wrought-iron grillwork that enclosed the galleries. Discreetly spaced lantern lights provided a soft illumination without hampering the velvety darkness that had spread across the sky and turned on the stars. The chirrup of crickets and locusts serenaded the scattering of guests on the veranda as they conversed in hushed voices in the quiet of the night.

Trace stepped outside for a smoke and to escape the endless talk. Every time he turned around, it seemed he was being cornered by someone and obliged to listen to the same propositions, the same complaints, or the same gossip.

Pausing in the shadows, he bent his head to the cupped match flame and let his gaze wander over the dimly lit veranda. It stopped when he noticed Pilar standing against the backdrop of a fluted white column. The Silvertons were there as well but she was off to one side, engaged in a private conversation with a chestnut-haired man Trace had met earlier in the evening. It was the same man she'd sat next to at dinner when he had finally managed to find her.

The softness of her laughter came to him across the distance. It unsettled him to see the way she was smiling at that man, intent on his every word, it seemed. The man's name escaped Trace, but he was some attorney-friend of Silverton's. The man made a gesture with the glass in his hand, then headed for the doors Trace had just exited through, evidently intending to get another drink. Trace waited a minute, then strolled toward Pilar.

"Some escort you are," she declared with mock reproach when he walked up to her. "You bring me to this party and then you forget me." She was only half teasing, reminding herself that she hadn't expected him to spend every minute by her side.

"I saw you a couple of times and started to come over, but you didn't appear to be lacking company." His lazy glance didn't quite hide the traveling inspection of his eyes before his attention wandered to the veranda doors of the south parlor. "Have you been enjoying yourself?"

"Yes, I have." Which was true, so there wasn't any reason to pretend otherwise. "I did look for you after dinner, but I always seemed to be one step behind you. Everyone kept telling me they'd just seen you someplace else, so I decided you had to be having a fairly good time."

"That depends." He pulled on his cigarette and exhaled the smoke, his mouth quirking dryly. "So far I've been invited to join nearly every civic and business organization in town."

"Is that good or bad?" Pilar couldn't help smiling.

"It's respectable," he countered.

She laughed in her throat. "Is that a yes or a no?"

"A no," Trace replied. "You can carry a good thing too far."

"So I've heard." She was amused by his droll but honest response. There was a warm feeling, too. After what had happened, she hadn't expected to feel so relaxed with him. Not that she was totally relaxed. There was still a kind of "alive" sensitivity to her nerves, a pleasing tingle of awareness.

"I noticed you were talking to Silverton's friend when I came outside." Again Trace took a drag on his cigarette and squinted at the smoke that curled upward. "Have you known him long?"

"You mean Ben Grafton?" In the course of a discussion about occupations and mutual interests, Pilar had learned his last name. He'd given her his business card. "I just met him tonight, but he seems nice . . . and fun to be with."

"I imagine his wife and two children in Memphis would agree with you." His glance ran over her sobering expression. "Or hasn't he gotten around to mentioning his family yet?"

"No, he hasn't," she admitted and breathed in deeply. "It seems I omitted asking a fairly important question. Maybe I should have you fill in my party program," she murmured in an absent reference to a bygone era when unattached women had cards, allotting a dance or portion of the evening to certain eligible males.

"That might not be a good idea." Trace looked away, briefly arching an eyebrow. "My name might be the only one you'd find written down. And you wouldn't like that, would you?" His glance swung back to her, something intimate and challenging in the dark gray depths of his eyes.

A sense of rising expectancy seemed to well

in her throat, strangling off any reply that she might have made. It disturbed her . . . *Trace* disturbed her. And she realized that she had falsely believed they were conversing on a platonic plane that didn't exist. They had been almost lovers, but never friends. Had she thought they could?

Agitation twisted her stomach into little knots as she broke free of his lazy, probing gaze. She looked anywhere but at him, struggling against the restlessness that charged her nerves and took the pleasure out of the evening.

The cigarette butt was buried in the earthen bed of a large stone urn, positioned by the towering white column. "How much longer do you want to stay here?" Trace inquired with an effortless change of subject and tempo.

"I'm ready to leave whenever you are." The social evening had lost its charm for her. Now the time would begin to drag.

"Then why don't we say our good-byes and leave?" he suggested.

At her nod of agreement, his hand lightly fitted itself to the small of her back to guide her. Even though there was an impersonal quality to his touch, it was innately possessive. She couldn't ignore the sensation of it.

It was a long process to work their way around to speak to various friends and locate the members of the committee that had hosted the dinner. Finally they reached the wide, dividing hall, and the door was in sight.

When Trace spied the silver-haired matriarch holding court in the middle of the hall under its elaborately carved arch, he muttered an aside to Pilar. "I suppose we have to say good night to the old 'battleaxe.'"

"She's president of the club. We certainly do." Her voice was equally low, and sharply reproving for his less than complimentary description of Catherine Braymore.

There were times when the matron of the community was overly condescending or patronizing, never suffering fools gladly, but she was also highly competent at organizing benefits and fund raisers such as tonight's dinner and seeing them through to a successful conclusion. She was irritating at times, but Pilar still admired her.

Her smile was slightly fixed in place, however, when she approached the buxom woman in pale lavender. "Good evening, Mrs. Braymore. The dinner was a success . . . as usual."

"Why, thank you, my dear." She pressed Pilar's hand between her ringed fingers. "It did go well. And I appreciate the help you gave us." Her attention switched to Trace, her expression becoming a little distant. "I am pleased you are finally doing your duty and escorting your stepmother to these functions, Trace. It's time you began to show her some respect after ignoring her for so long and leaving her to fend for herself."

Pilar felt him stiffen at the censure. Then

his hand came away from her back, and the contact was broken. She darted him a sidelong glance and noticed the coldness of his smile.

"You are still the same as I remembered you, Mrs. Braymore. Someday you'll have to tell me how you do it." It was a lazy, drawling response, riddled with mockery.

"I was told you had changed, but I see they were mistaken," she declared with a heavy sigh that seemed to say he wasn't worth the trouble he caused.

"How can you say that, Mrs. Braymore?" Trace chided her dryly. "I've been on my best behavior all evening."

"With you it rarely lasts." Yet her expression seemed indulgent. "Now, run along. And see that your stepmother arrives home safely."

"You can be sure I'll do that, Mrs. Braymore." His tone was so cynical that Pilar shot a worried glance at him. There was a hard and ominous glitter in his eyes. "As a matter of fact, I can almost guarantee it."

The tension fairly crackled around him as they walked toward the door. Pilar had to hurry to keep up with his quick, reaching strides. He held the door open for her with marked patience, then followed her out. He seemed caught up in his own thoughts, not giving her more than perfunctory attention. He didn't even bother to open the car door for her, letting her climb in by herself while he slid behind the wheel and started the motor.

"You shouldn't have let the things she said rile you," Pilar finally commented when the silence became intolerable.

"I've been told that's one of my problems." The curtness in his voice didn't encourage conversation.

When they reached the house, Pilar didn't wait for Trace to get out of the car to open her door. "Thank you for the ride," she said into the brooding silence and climbed out of the passenger side.

Before climbing the fan-shaped steps to the darkened porch, she opened her purse and extracted the door key. Her pulse made a startled leap at the sudden slam of the car door. With the key in hand, she started up the steps, aware of the footsteps that followed her. His shadow loomed beside hers as she crossed the board floor to the heavy doors.

"It isn't necessary to walk me to the door," she said.

"I insist."

At the door Pilar inserted the key in the lock and turned it. There was the snap of an unlocking bolt. She pushed the heavy door partway open, then turned to face him, blocking the opening with her body.

"I did enjoy this evening, Trace." It was a quietly voiced statement that didn't give the words any special meaning. They were polite and sincere but no more than that.

"Mrs. Braymore was right, you know." In the shadows cast by the porch, it was difficult to see his features. "No matter how good my intentions are, they rarely last."

For a minute she thought his ill humor had vanished until she felt the pinioning grip of his hands on her arms that bound them to her side while they hauled her nearer. After a split second of shock she managed to bring her hands up and push them at his chest.

"Tell me something, Pilar." He seemed amused, in a distantly complacent way, by her look of anger. "What do you suppose the good people of Natchez would think if they knew I was going to kiss my 'stepmommy' good night?"

Pilar recoiled from the bitterness in his voice and the sordid-sounding words, but there was no eluding the mouth that drove itself onto hers, forcing her head back until she thought her neck would snap from the pressure. Her lips were ground against her teeth in a kiss that was all anger and brute force.

Her fingers curled into the lapels of his jacket as she strained away from him, pushing with all her strength, but she gained nothing except to make his bruising fingers dig more deeply into her flesh. The blood hammered in her head, pounding with the excruciating pressure. Blackness was reeling on the edges of her consciousness from the lack of air.

Trace broke it off as abruptly as he'd begun

the kiss. For an instant she sagged in the support of his hands and tried to gather in air for her starved lungs. Then her fingers gingerly touched bloodless lips. Tears sprang in her eyes, making them sparkle with wet brilliance when she finally looked at him.

"Why, Trace?" Her choked voice was barely louder than a breath. "Why do you have to destroy everything? Why do you have to hurt people?"

Deep lines of regret were carved into his rugged features. The hand that touched her cheek was incredibly gentle. Slowly he bent his head and pressed his mouth onto her forehead. "I'm sorry." He mouthed the words against her skin.

This controlled gesture of affection reminded Pilar of a grown son kissing his mother. The anger that flared was nothing like the wounded hurt she'd felt before. She shoved away from him.

"Stop it," she ordered, incensed by his action. "I'm not your mother . . . or your stepmother! And I won't be treated like one!"

There was an instant of silence. Then Trace tilted his head back, his throat a patch of lighter gold in the porch shadows, and laughed with very little humor in the sound.

"My God, that's rich, Pilar," he declared, still chuckling harshly. "I could never treat you like a mother. That's been my problem all along."

She was left standing on the porch as his long frame glided down the steps to the car. There were a great many things she saw more clearly. Yet they all seemed to tangle her emotions into a confused knot.

Chapter Eight

$\mathcal{A}$ half-hearted attempt had been made to clean the serving tray of solid silver, but the tarnish was still embedded in the intricate design on its flat surface. Inch by inch Pilar rubbed the silver cleaner into the tray and watched the intricacy of the pineapple motif unfold. The pineapple had been a popular symbol of hospitality in the Old South, carved into furniture and silver and painted on china.

"I can't believe they auctioned this service as silver-*plated*." She murmured her good fortune at snaring such a bargain. "Of course, there were so many items at that estate sale, and no family to know the worth of what was being sold. But you'd think they would have had someone appraise things before they started selling them."

"That tray looked so ugly when you brought it in, I thought you'd made some kind of mistake," Cassie declared, pausing to look over Pilar's shoulder at the progress she was making. "It's going to be a beautiful piece."

"I have half a notion to keep it." Pilar straightened and flexed her fingers, cramped from all the rubbing. "But the antique business is buying and selling. You don't make any money to pay the overhead by collecting."

"I'm sure that's true." Cassie slipped a coffee cup off the mug tree on the counter, then reached for the second. "Would you like a cup of coffee?"

"I'd love one." Pilar wiped her blackened fingers on a rag and leaned back in the wooden straight-backed chair to take a break. "It's a warm night, isn't it?" She lifted the weight of her hair off her neck and let the blowing air from the window fan cool her skin.

"It's been hotter, but the thick walls of this house keep out most of the heat," Cassie commented and brought the full coffee cups to the kitchen table. "In the heat of the summer Trace always used to beg to sleep outside on the porch. He swore he didn't care if the bugs carried him away in the night. He claimed it was too hot in his room, but it was just an excuse to go running and tearing around all night long. He thought if he was sleeping on the porch, no one would hear him slip off." A smile pushed dimples into her cheeks. "And most of the time no one did. That boy," she declared with a shake of her head. "The things he didn't do."

"Why was he such a rebel?" It was a question she'd put to Trace, and he'd managed to change the subject before she had an answer.

"I don't think you can look back and lay your finger on any one thing," Cassie replied thoughtfully. "Being an only child put a lot of expectations on him that had to put a strain on him. And his mother dying when he was in those awkward years didn't help. I think for a long time he was angry with her for passing on and leaving him alone. 'Course, Elliot said that Trace got into so much trouble just to draw attention to himself. And I suppose there's some truth in that, too."

"I often wondered whether he resented my marriage to Elliot." Pilar offered it as an idle comment, but she watched the black woman closely for a reaction.

"Well, I couldn't say about that." Cassie took a sip of her coffee. "But I don't believe he objected to the idea of his father getting married again. After Trace turned about sixteen, he went his way and Elliot went the other. His mother seemed to be the link that held them together. When she was gone, they didn't have much in common."

"Does he take after his mother?"

"He has her coloring and strong features. She was a handsome woman and . . . yes, a little on the unconventional side. I didn't know her well until the disease had progressed to the point where she needed constant care, but"—Cassie paused, frowning absently—"I do remember her telling me some stories about their early years of marriage, and how embarrassed Elliot would get over some of the improper things she said in public. It could be that she was just as much of a rebel at heart as Trace is, but being a woman—and in those times—she kept it all inside." She started chuckling. "I could just picture her burning her brassiere in the street. She would have done that, to the mortification of all the good ladies of Natchez."

"She sounds like quite a lady." Pilar had often wondered about Elliot's first wife, but he hadn't wanted to talk about her.

She had been reluctant to ask Cassie about her since she didn't know the woman well. Later her curiosity had faded, until now when she wanted to find out more about Trace's mother. How strange, she thought to herself, she was thinking of the woman as Trace's mother instead of Elliot's first wife.

"She was. There was always a bit of jealousy between Trace and Elliot over her. There used to be quite a competition between them. 'Course it all changed when she died. They stopped competing *with* each other and started competing *against* each other. And that's when all the trouble started." Cassie studied her with a critical eye. "You look tired. Why don't you leave that tray until tomorrow and finish it then?"

"I can't." Pilar picked up the rag and began to rub again. "There's a sale tomorrow afternoon outside of Port Gibson I want to attend."

"You've been going constantly."

"Look who's talking." Pilar chided the woman's own full schedule. "They always seem to hold more auctions in the summer. The weather's better and they draw more people, I guess. It's a good thing I have competent help in the shop so I can catch some of these weekday sales without having to close the store."

It was midmorning when Pilar stopped at the antique shop, simply named the Antique Corner, for a last-minute check with Florence Barslow before leaving town. There had been one inquiry for a particular medicine bottle, which Florence had been able to refer to a dealer who specialized in antique bottles.

"I cleaned this up last night." Pilar unwrapped the tissue protecting the silver tray. "You might want to put some complementing pieces with it and arrange it on that banquet table if you have free time today."

"I will." The older woman was skilled at displaying pieces to their best advantage. "Don't forget to keep an eye out for a chair to match Mrs. Aulderson's dining room table set."

"I won't." The long strap of her purse was

pushed higher onto her shoulder as she gathered up her leather briefcase-pouch containing her notes, papers, and a list of items clients had indicated an interest in purchasing. "See you tomorrow, and wish me luck."

The bell above the door tinkled as she walked out into the street. Her glance ran absently to the man standing in front of her shop window. Pilar halted with a bit of a jolt when she recognized Trace. His jacket was hanging over his shoulder and a hand was thrust nonchalantly in a pocket.

"Hello." Trace spoke first and glanced at the window display. "The business looks prosperous."

"It is," she assured him. "Go inside and take a look around. We welcome browsers."

"I've seen it before." A slow smile touched the corners of his mouth at the dubious look on her face. "You were away somewhere."

"Oh." Florence probably hadn't thought it was important to mention. "Well, I'm off again today." She smiled quickly at him and started for the compact car parked at the curb.

"Where are you going?" Trace angled away from the window to follow her.

"An auction north of town," she explained and walked around the car to the driver's side. After opening the door, she tossed her purse and leather pouch onto the opposite seat.

"Mind if I come along?"

Pilar straightened, not sure that she could possibly have heard him correctly. She stared at him across the roof of the car. His steady gaze didn't waver, the faint question staying in his expression.

"I'll be gone for the rest of the day," she pointed out to him, faltering in vague confusion. "You . . . you have to be at the office."

"Haven't you ever heard of playing hookey?" Trace chided.

"But you're in charge." His suggestion sounded so irresponsible that Pilar was dumbfounded, doubting that he was serious and wondering if he was. "You can't just walk away."

"Can't I?" He opened the passenger door and threw his jacket into the back seat. "If the boss can't take a day off when he wants it, who can? Besides, I'll go stir-crazy if I have to sit behind that desk for the rest of the morning and afternoon."

"You're welcome to come along." Since he had already invited himself, her agreement to the arrangement seemed almost superfluous. Pilar crawled behind the wheel and fished her purse and case out of his seat so he could get in. "But don't blame me if you get bored."

"Boredom would be a pleasant change of pace," he declared dryly and folded his long length into the compact quarters.

"Do you want me to drive by the office so you can let them know you won't be back?" The motor rumbled when she turned the ignition key, then hummed steadily.

"No."

"Trace—" Pilar began.

"Are you trying to be my conscience?" He interrupted with a half-amused look. "All right," he conceded partially. "I'll call when we reach this place we're going. Believe me, they'll be relieved to have me off their backs for the rest of the day."

"I thought things were going smoothly." She glanced at him as Trace leaned back in the seat and made use of the elevated head-rest. Strain and tension had left tracks in his bronzed features, creasing its leanness.

"With the business they are." His eyes were closed. "It's just everything else that's lousy." There was a small pause. "I don't mean to destroy things—or to hurt anyone."

Those were the words she had used last week when he'd kissed her with such cruelty. Her fingers nervously clenched at the steering wheel, flexing and tightening their grip on it. With an effort Pilar kept her gaze fixed on the road, struggling with all the raw emotions that churned inside her.

"Pilar."

"Yes." All her attention stayed on the traffic.

"I had no right to take my frustration out on you. So you have my apology."

Under the circumstances she felt obligated to reciprocate as magnanimously as he had. "It's forgotten."

She turned onto the parkway out of Natchez and headed north. Not once did Trace ask their destination as they traveled along the scenic highway. At nearly every bend in the picturesque, tree-lined road, there was a historic marker. They passed Emerald Mound, an ancient temple mound built hundreds of years ago by some unknown tribe of Indians.

Once Trace commented, "My mother named me after the Natchez Trace. There was a time when I believed that this long trail had put the restless wanderlust in me."

Cars of spectators and buyers were already arriving at the auction when Pilar located the turnoff to the old, rambling house. She parked the car where it would have afternoon shade on it, then gathered her things from the rear seat.

"When does it start?" Trace stepped out and stretched his cramped back and shoulders.

"Not for another hour and a half," she answered. "But I like to come early and look over the items before they're put on the block. I told you," she reminded him, her lips slanting in a faint smile, "you might get bored."

"We'll see." He didn't appear concerned and trailed after her when she went to the registration table to sign up and receive her number.

Most of the larger items were sitting in the side lawn. Pilar took her time wandering through their maze, stopping for a closer look at a particular item or to examine the manufacturer's mark. Several times she paused to poke through boxes of dishes and knickknacks. All along the way she jotted down notes.

"What are you writing?" Trace attempted to read her scribbling, but it was her own indecipherable brand of shorthand.

"There was some Depression glass in that one box. I was just making a note of it. Of course, one of the larger bowls had a chip in it."

"That sounds like sour grapes."

"I guess it is," she laughed briefly. "I can always console myself with the knowledge that there was a chip in it if someone else gets it besides me. But it's little things like that which alter the value of a piece."

"Yes, I've noticed how thorough you are, grubbing through those boxes like a packrat," he observed and let his gaze slide down to the grass stains on the knees of her denim jeans. "I also understand why you're wearing jeans and a cotton shirt."

"If I want to look at something, I don't want to worry about getting my clothes dirty. This might not be fashionable," she admitted, glancing down at the slim-fitting jeans, "but it sure saves on the cleaning bill." As her glance came up, she happened to look over his shoulder and spied a tall chifforobe. "Look at that," she breathed quickly. "It looks like a mate to that four-poster bed Mrs. Kenyon owns over in Hattiesburg."

Eager to confirm it, she fumbled with her notepad and pencil while she tried to open the pouch for the list. Finally she shoved part of it into Trace's hands to rummage for the customer list.

"Is it?" he asked.

"Let's go take a look at it," she said and chewed thoughtfully at her lip.

"It appears someone else is interested in it, too." Trace drew her attention to the couple who were standing back to study it and talking between themselves.

"Yes." Pilar took no notice of them as she walked over to the chifforobe, opening its drawers and doors and checking on various details. Then she stepped back to stand next to Trace.

"It looks to be in pretty good shape," he commented.

"It's too bad the drawer pulls and handles don't match. They aren't the original ones anyway so I guess it doesn't matter," she declared. "The doors are warped, too. Did you notice the way they nailed a board on the back to brace that rear leg?"

"No, I didn't notice that." Trace eyed her with the beginnings of a gleam.

"It's a beautiful piece of furniture." Her deep sigh was heavy with regret as Pilar ran an absently stroking hand over the wood's smooth patina. "It's a shame anyone let it get in this condition."

All her comments were taken in by the eavesdropping couple who had been initially admiring the chifforobe, and the avid excitement that had been in their expressions began to fade. They exchanged a look, and the man shrugged faintly in apparent dismissal. Together they moved with reluctance onto the next item.

"You're a calculating woman." Trace chuckled in his throat. "Those are just minor things, right?"

One shoulder lifted in an expressive shrug as Pilar made some quick notes on her ringed tablet. "They are obviously amateur collectors. I would never have been able to fool a dealer. Maybe this way, the price will stay reasonable. Private buyers, especially the ones who aren't knowledgeable, usually drive the price up and pay more for something than it's worth." Finished, she looked up and met his amused study of her.

"So you conned them." He murmured the accusation without any criticism.

The small, rueful smile that touched the corners of her lips was only faintly apologetic. "Maybe I saved them some money," Pilar suggested. "All's fair in the antique business."

"So I'm learning."

After checking the description of the next item on the sales list, Pilar wandered over to examine it. On the surface she gave her attention to her work, but Trace's presence at her side gave a little edge of excitement to the afternoon. She knew when he was watching her or standing close to read her notes. All her senses seemed finely tuned to him.

Before the auction started, Trace left her to locate a telephone and called his office. Pilar retreated to the shade of a tree to sit on the grass and used the trunk for a backrest while she refined her notes, the pad balanced on her bent knees.

When Trace rejoined her, the auctioneer had already begun his rhythmic spiel to exhort bids from the large crowd on the first item, but Pilar was still sitting under the tree. He crouched down, rocking onto his heels, and idly plucked a blade of grass to chew on.

His arrival briefly distracted her from the last-minute checklist she was making. In case he was wondering, she explained absently, "The first items are almost always small, unimportant stuff—to warm up the crowd and allow time for all the latecomers to arrive. They save the best until last to keep as many people as long as they can." Pilar tucked the papers she wouldn't be needing into the leather pouch and rolled to her feet with an assisting pull from Trace. "I warned you we'd be all afternoon," she reminded him again.

"I'm not complaining." There was a disturbing darkness in the gray of his eyes as he looked down at her.

The rhythm of her pulse became slightly erratic. Making an effort to steady it, she moved away from him and led the way into the semicircle of bidders until she found a space that gave her a good vantage point of the proceedings.

A hot wind kept the air circulating and prevented the afternoon heat from becoming oppressive and stifling. Several times Pilar sent a glance over her shoulder at Trace, who had taken a position slightly behind her, just to see if he was still there. But as the afternoon wore on and the items she was most interested in came up for bid, her concentration centered more and more on the auctioneer and her various competitors for an item. There were a few familiar faces she recognized in the crowd, other dealers like herself.

Although she bid on many items, she was successful on less than a handful. When the bidding went higher than she thought the piece was worth, Pilar dropped out of it. Happily the chifforobe wasn't among the items she lost.

The satisfaction that came from knowing it had been a successful day more than made up for the tension that came from all the intense bidding. Details had to be handled before she could savor her success. The items had to be paid for, bills of sale obtained, and arrangements made to transport them to her store.

When the last transaction had been completed, she was finally able to turn to Trace and announce, "I'm all done."

There was a radiance to her face, her dark eyes shining with that inner glow of satisfaction. She was oblivious to the heat that had her cotton blouse sticking to her damp skin and profiling the roundly jutting contours of her breasts.

The running wind had made a black tangle of her shoulder-length hair, tousling its curling thickness in attractive disarray. But it was more than the allure of her looks or body that made it so difficult for Trace to take his eyes off her. It was her sparkle and vitality, the inner flame that pulled him.

Taking a grip on his senses, Trace forced a tight smile onto his mouth. "Do you think we can make it to the car without being run over in this traffic jam?" He made a light reference to the confusion of vehicles all trying to leave at once.

"We can try," she said with an exuberant lilt in her voice.

Automatically Trace took her hand to negotiate the moving maze of cars turning and reversing and trying to meld into an exit line. There was a lightness about the way she moved, a bounce and a glide that seemed filled with a zesty lust for life.

"Want me to drive?" Trace asked when they finally reached her compact auto, parked in the long shadow of an oak.

"Sure." Pilar slipped her hand from his grasp and dug out the car keys from the bottom of her purse. They jangled as she dropped them in his outstretched palm and then split away from him to walk to the passenger side.

After sitting all afternoon in the summer heat, the car's interior was stuffy and suffocatingly close. Hurriedly Pilar rolled the window down to let out some of the hot, stale air and allow some circulation.

When Trace started the engine, she adjusted the vent openings so the full force of the blowing air was directed at her. With both hands she lifted the weight of her hair off her neck, then shook it loose. All the while the small smile of satisfaction continued to soften the curve of her lips.

"You're looking very pleased with yourself," Trace observed while he waited for an opening in the stream of cars.

"I am," she said with a contented and happy sigh. Her dark eyes were bright with the same feelings when she looked at him. "It was a good day. I suppose you're glad it's over."

"Sorry to disappoint you, but I enjoyed myself." A car slowed and made a place for him in the exiting line of vehicles.

"Really?" She was faintly skeptical that he was sincere.

"Yes, really." Trace smiled. "Especially watching the way you wheeled and bluffed and tried to maneuver the bidding. You're good at it."

Pilar turned her face to the rush of wind that blew in through the open window. Almost absently she remembered, "It would have driven Elliot up a wall to spend an entire afternoon attending an auction."

"Why?"

"Oh . . . he wanted me to buy everything I bid on, regardless of how high it went." The tone of a dismissing shrug was in her voice as she rested an elbow on the sill and combed fingers through her hair in an absent fashion. "It used to drive him crazy when someone topped my bid and I wouldn't say more."

"He liked to win," Trace agreed blandly.

"Yes, but sometimes when you win, you lose," Pilar stated.

"I've been in a few no-win situations, so I know what you're talking about." Practically all of the traffic was taking the road that lead to the main highway, but Trace turned in the opposite direction. "Sometimes when there's no way to win, you have to decide the best way to lose."

"Where are you going?" Pilar realized he'd turned the wrong way.

"I thought we'd beat the traffic and use one of the back roads." He looked around the countryside as if seeking a familiar landmark. "It's been a while since I was here, but I think this road takes us past the Windsor ruins."

His remark prompted her to make a sweep of the surrounding landscape. A couple of miles farther down the road, they came upon the remains of the once magnificent mansion and Trace slowed the car, finally braking to a stop.

A collection of giant, Corinthian columns, towering four stories into the air, stood forlornly in an empty field. They were left behind to mark the site where the antebellum house had once stood. Like silent sentinels they stood, twenty-two of the original twenty-nine massive pillars that had once fronted the mansion on four sides.

Underbrush and trees had grown up around them as the land struggled to reclaim what belonged to it. The long, golden rays of a setting sun aged them with a yellow light and stretched their shadows over the ground. Time and the elements had chipped and peeled at the architectural moldings that adorned the lofty stone columns.

"It's sadly beautiful, isn't it?" Pilar murmured as she gazed at the imposing yet desolate ruins.

"Shall we go have a closer look?" Trace made the suggestion as he switched off the motor and climbed out of the car.

Pilar was slower to follow his lead, stepping out of the passenger side and hesitating by the door. "It's all fenced. I don't think whoever owns it now wants people poking around there."

"We'll live dangerously and trespass." He took her firmly by the hand and half pulled her along with him into the tall grass with his customary disregard for rules. "I'll pay the fine if we're caught."

"You're impossible." But she laughed when she said it, caught up in the excitement of actually walking among the massive columns.

The long tangle of grass made walking difficult, especially when she had trouble watching where she was going. Her glance kept looking up and up at the columns, which seemed to grow bigger and higher the closer they came. Trace climbed partway up the surrounding fence and vaulted the rest of the way, then waited to lift her to the ground when she topped the fence.

The grip of his hands on her waist was firm and strong, effortlessly lowering her to the solidness of the ground. Long after he'd taken them away, Pilar could feel the warm imprint of them. That disturbed edge to her senses was creeping back again.

Together they waded through the underbrush to the square base of the nearest column. Pilar had to crane her neck way back in order to see the ornate carvings at the top, forty-five feet in the air. A hot wind rustled through the ruins, seeming a moaning whisper from the past. There was an eerie splendor to the place that awed and hushed. Pieces of grillwork to an upper-floor balcony were still in place, connecting several of the columns on one side.

"It was destroyed by fire, wasn't it?" It had been a while since she'd heard the story of the Windsor mansion, so her memory wasn't clear on how it had happened. Pilar noticed traces of charring in the rubble as they strolled in the looming shadows.

"Yes." His gaze seemed to narrow in recollection of the tale, and she paused expectantly to listen to it again. "During the Civil War, General Grant refused to burn it, so it survived the great conflict to suffer a more inglo-

rious fate. At a party, somewhere around
1890 I believe, a guest tossed a smoldering
butt of one of those new tailored cigarettes
into a pile of wood shavings left behind by
carpenters hired to do some remodeling. It
burned to the ground in less than an hour."

Chapter Nine

The wind whipped at her hair, and Pilar shook the strands out of her face. Either her imagination was very vivid or the smell of smoke actually still lingered among the ruins. She leaned backward to rest against the solid base of a tall Corinthian column. Its surface still held the heat of the sun.

Her glance strayed to Trace and found him watching her. As if to conceal it, he shifted his position slightly and looked around at the encircling ruins. Absently he reached into his shirt pocket for a cigarette.

"Don't smoke." Pilar straightened from the column and laid a hand on his arm to halt his action. "It seems wrong."

Slowly he took his hand away from his pocket and turned to face her, his gaze burrowing into her with some fierce kind of need. Pilar drew back from it, not frightened, but hesitant, until she was again leaning against the sun-heated column. Trace followed her, leaning forward to brace a hand on the chiseled base by her head.

"What about us, Pilar?" His fingertips touched the underside of her jaw, lightly stroking it. "Does it seem wrong to you?"

She breathed in and couldn't breathe out, the tight little pain in her throat throttling off her air. She could only look at him, mute and hurting, without being sure of the cause. Tremors of longing shook her as she stared at the blunt ridges and hollows of his deeply tanned face. Dark lashes hooded the velvet intensity of his eyes, and the careless wind had trailed strands of black hair onto his forehead.

"I have to know." There was a huskiness in his voice as he relaxed the straightness of his arm and eased himself closer to her. His caressing fingers glided to the curve of her neck while his warm breath flowed over her sensitive facial skin. "I've wanted you for a long time, Pilar . . . from the day I met you at the wedding. I went away but the memory of you went with me."

His fingers were behind her neck and in her hair. She felt weak and boneless, incapable of movement. The strong, hard feel of his body leaned onto her, warming her flesh with its heat. Her long lashes fluttered downward as his mouth brushed her temple and stayed there, a hairsbreadth away, making her conscious of the movement of his lips when he spoke.

"I daydreamed about you—and night-dreamed, too." The muffled ache in his low voice throbbed through her. "You'll never know how many times I've made love to you in my mind. I tried to stay away, but it didn't seem to matter how many times I told myself that you couldn't belong to me, that it wasn't right to want you. I couldn't stop." He nuzzled her cheek and the corner of an eye, unleashing little shivers to dance over her skin. "Tell me to go away and never come near you again. Tell me it's wrong. But for God's sake, tell me something, Pilar!"

The groan in his voice quaked through her and ignited an ache that made thinking impossible. It was all turmoil inside as her senses took over, heightening her awareness of the hard, muscular thighs tautly pressed to her hips and legs.

There was something in his voice that seemed to be urging her to jump from some high place and promising he'd catch her. But the fear was that he wouldn't catch her and she'd just keep falling. Yet the insistence of his body was there, trying to make her decide to take that leap.

"I'm trying," was all she could moan.

Her inability to give him an answer, in itself, was an answer. The torment of having his mouth so close and not having his kisses finally ended as he covered her lips with a muffled sound, rent by an agony of longing. The rhythmic, rocking pressure of his mouth prized her lips apart so he could lick at their sensitive insides and tease the quivering tautness of her tongue.

Her flesh and bones seemed to turn into molten wax, all heated and pliant, fitting themselves to the impression of his hard, male shape. Everything was spinning; up and down became as irrelevant as right and wrong. This time Pilar couldn't pretend that alcohol had removed all her inhibitions to permit her to respond to a man's advances. She was abandoning herself to her own desires and wants, arousing and being aroused.

His long body pinned her to the stone pedestal as Trace flattened himself against her, as if to keep them from being whirled into some black space. The wildness was growing, reckless urges leading her to the edge. Pilar teetered, wanting to let go, yet not trusting her judgment.

With a twist of her head, she broke free of his kiss and pressed her forehead to his shoulder. Her heart was pounding in her throat, and the hands that had been embracing him became taut little fists of mute resistance.

"Please, let me stop." She was half-sobbing the demand.

There was an instant of rigidity, a silent rebellion by Trace that any of the onus should be placed on him. Yet something in her air of vulnerability aroused the male instinct to protect.

Relief shuddered rawly through her when he eased the physical pressure of his body, albeit with obvious reluctance. His arms gathered her away from the pedestal and held her with taut gentleness. His hand trembled slightly as it stroked her hair.

For long seconds she let him hold her while she cried silently and inwardly. Through his shirt she could feel the heat of his skin and the heavy thudding of his heart. The smell of him was hot and heady, like a rich wine that had sat in the sun.

"I don't know how much longer I can go on like this, Pilar." His mouth moved against the silken texture of her ebony hair. "Wanting you and not having you."

The comfort of his arms suddenly became a torment. With a jerkiness that seemed at odds with her natural grace, Pilar turned out of them and took a quick step away. Feeling oddly cold without the heat of his body to warm her, she clutched at her arms and hugged them tightly. The hot summer wind whipped at her, lashing long strands of hair to sting her face. Her eyes smarted with tears but she didn't cry.

There was a faint sound behind her. She sucked in her breath at the light touch of his hands on her shoulders. Tactile and restless, they traveled down her arms and slipped onto the front of her taut stomach. The outline of his body began to make its impression down the length of her spine and her tensed bottom.

"I don't know which is worse, Pilar." He rubbed his chin and jaw against her hair. "Being away from you or being near you. Both of them are hell."

"Don't say any more," she protested on a taut whisper. "Don't make it impossible for me to—" Her mind seemed to go blank, unable to find the words to finish the sentence as his hands slid under her crossed arms to cup the underswell of her breasts.

"To what? To be with me?" There was a roughness to his low voice, a faint note of derision that she hadn't realized it was already impossible.

Her fingers pulled at his wrists to tug his hands from their evocative possession of her breasts. "Don't." She moved out of his destroying hold and swung around to eye him warily while she ached inside. "You touch me and it's all confusion."

"Is that bad?" There was something hungry and needing about the way he looked at her and it nearly shoved her back into his arms.

All that want was on a chain and the links were stretching. Yet Pilar couldn't answer with any certainty in her heart. Between them lay the long shadow of a towering column, a symbol of something from the past that was over and dead.

An anger seemed to wash through him,

transposing that stillness into a restless energy that pushed him into movement and directed his reaching strides away from her. "You don't have to say anything," he muttered testily. "It's plain what you think of me, and God knows I never claimed my morals were above reproach." In two more strides he was at the fence. The wires groaned as he made a quick climb to the top and vaulted to the opposite side, then turned to impatiently eye her. "Come on. Let's get back to the car."

Some invisible force seemed to draw her slowly to the fence where he waited. Pilar searched the bronzed tautness of his face, aware of the glittering reluctance of his gray eyes to meet her look. Her fingers curled onto the barbed wire, but she made no effort to climb it.

"You're wrong, Trace," she said quietly.

"About what?" he challenged in a short, stiff voice.

"My opinion of you," she replied. There was a slow movement of her head that swayed it from side to side. "Whatever I may have thought about you before, it's changed. Sometimes I wonder if you don't deliberately act tough and uncaring so others don't discover how strong and sensitive you are."

"Don't go making romantic images of me in your mind," Trace warned tersely. "I'm not a dashing hero. You're mixing me up with my father."

"Am I?" Pilar came back with a calm,

steady response. "Earlier . . . you stopped. You didn't want to—you didn't have to—but you did."

He stepped closer to the barrier of barbed wire that separated them. It would have been a simple matter to reach through and touch him, but the gray smolder in his eyes kept her motionless.

"You waited until there was a fence between us before you told me that. You know why, don't you? Because you don't trust me enough to wait until you had climbed over it." There was a sharp bite to his tone. "Before you implant some noble interpretation in your mind about the reason I stopped, I'll explain. It's simple, really. Rape wasn't what I had in mind. I was thinking more along the lines of spending a solid week in bed with you. It'd take at least that long to take the ache out of my system, and even then, it wouldn't be enough." Pilar blanched slightly, unnerved by his candor. His mouth twisted into a cold smile at her reaction. "That's more in keeping with my crass character, isn't it? It rather wrecks the genteel image you tried to give me, doesn't it?"

"Not in the way you think." But it was a subdued response as she stepped onto the bottom wire to crawl over the fence.

Trace didn't help her this time, leaving her to manage on her own. But he waited, impatience seeming to ripple under the surface, his silence like an angry riptide. When her feet touched the ground on the other side,

Pilar turned to face him, raising her chin slightly.

"Someday maybe you can explain to me why you feel you have to deny that streak of decency," she stated and started through the tall grass toward the car.

In a stride Trace was walking abreast of her and the impersonal touch of his hand was on her back, lightly steering her across the field. His chin was thrust forward at a hard, decisive angle while a grim silence ruled his expression. When they reached the car, he opened the door for her and held it. The steely gleam in his eye bothered her, and he hesitated at climbing in.

"All right, Pilar," he said in a kind of challenge. "If that's what it takes, we'll do it your way."

"What do you mean?" She eyed him, leery of his mood and his statement.

"I got your signals crossed and thought you wanted to be rushed into an affair. I forgot that the first time you only had in mind a one-night stand."

"Did you have to bring that up?" She resented his reference to that disastrous night when she had secretly wanted to be seduced. "So much for your claim that it was forgotten," she declared bitterly and quickly slid into the passenger seat.

The door was pushed shut. Her darting gaze watched Trace walk around the hood of the car to the driver's side. He climbed in and angled his long body in the seat to face her, an arm resting on the top curve of the steering wheel.

"Be honest with yourself for once, Pilar," he insisted curtly. "You haven't forgotten it anymore than I have. It's colored every meeting we've had since it happened. After reaching that physical level, it's pretty damned hard to back off to innocent hand-holding."

"Trace—" Pilar struggled for some kind of denial while she stared straight ahead.

His thumb and forefinger caught her chin and turned it so she had to look at him. Within the deep intensity of his gaze, there was a gentleness that caught her.

"All right." The phrase of concession seemed to be forced from him. "You want to be courted," he stated. The line of his mouth was straight with the fierce check he had on his emotions. "I'll try."

There was a silent acknowledgment within her that Trace was right. She wanted to be courted, but not for the reason he probably suspected. There was no doubt in her mind that a strong sexual attraction existed, but she needed time to judge for herself whether it was right to let it develop into anything more.

His thumb slowly rubbed itself across her mouth, then followed the curved outline of her lips while his gaze tracked its movements with a disturbing interest.

"There's a brutal irony in this, Pilar," he murmured. "I refused to compete with my father when he was alive. Now I'm in a position where I have to compete with his ghost."

"No." The denial rushed from her, bringing a quick frown to her forehead.

His mouth twisted a little. "The hell it isn't so. He's haunting us, in one way or another." With her chin still resting on the crook of his finger, Trace leaned forward and took a kiss from her lips, as if making sure it was his image in her mind. Then he asked, "Will you have dinner with me tonight?"

"Yes." After the tantalizing warmth of his kiss, her acceptance came as easy as breathing.

"Good." He pulled back and squared around to start the car. "Where would you like to go? You name the place."

"There's a wayside restaurant on the highway not far from here. I've stopped there before. The food was always good. I'm not really dressed for anything else," she said in a subconscious defense of her choice.

"That's no problem." Trace gave her a considering look as the car started forward. "We can always stop by Dragon Walk so you can change clothes before we go out to eat."

Pilar had an answer ready for that. "I'd rather stop somewhere on the way home. It's been a long time since breakfast. By the time we drove all the way back and I changed clothes, it would be late."

"Whatever you say," he returned smoothly.

At the restaurant Pilar caught a glimpse of her reflection in the glass panes of the window front as they entered. After nearly all day exposed to the summer elements, she was a disheveled mess. Before they were seated at a table, she excused herself to go to the ladies' room and make the necessary repairs to her appearance with the odd bits of makeup in her purse.

When she rejoined Trace, her lips were shining with a fresh application of gloss, there was a dusting of blush on her cheekbones, and her dark hair was brushed until it glistened with blue-black lights. He was seated at a small table in a quiet corner of the restaurant. His gaze moved appreciatively over her, warming her in a way that was vaguely exciting.

"That was worth the wait," he murmured.

"Flattery won't get you anywhere." But there was a slightly pleased smile on her face as she picked up the menu that had been left at her place setting.

"I've tried nearly everything else. It was worth a chance." There was a dancing gleam in his glance, wicked and lively.

She pretended to study the menu. "What are you going to order?"

"I'm afraid what I want they don't have on the menu." It was in the suggestive tone of his voice that what he wanted was her.

Her gaze stayed glued to the menu print, but there was an odd little leaping of her pulse. "You're not making this easy, Trace." It was a low, taut murmur of protest.

"I don't want to make it easy," he replied. The table between them was small and narrow. It was unavoidable that their knees and legs would touch and Trace took full advantage of even this inadvertent contact. "I want to make it hard, so this farce can't continue for long."

"And what makes you so certain it won't become a tragedy?" Pilar challenged.

His expression became serious. "I'm not. And neither are you. That's why you want to turn the pages so slowly."

"And you don't." She couldn't help searching his face.

A reckless smile played with the corners of his mouth as he took her hand and wrapped it in the largeness of his. "No, I don't. I want to jump ahead and read the end."

There was a marveling shake of her head, a gesture tinged with a certain wryness. "I swear, Trace Santee, you love taking wild risks."

"I like knowing where I stand. I can take a 'no.' It's the maybes that are killing me." His thumb was absently rubbing circles in the center of her sensitive palm. It made her feel all raw inside. "There's only so long you can postpone a thing."

"I know." There was a breathiness to her voice and a lack of will to draw her hand away.

"How much longer do you think I'm going to have to be content with just holding your hand, Pilar?" he questioned huskily.

"Some relationships never progress out of that stage." She deliberately withheld any commitment to the future. It wasn't wise. There was too much chance that the whole thing would blow up in her face tomorrow.

"I won't buy that." His gaze traveled with familiar intimacy over the front of her blouse, the material lifting with the quick rise and fall of her breasts. "It isn't your hand you want me to hold."

His remark only increased the inner agitation she was trying to conceal. "I wish you would stop making love to me with words," she protested.

"I prefer the alternative to that myself." His smile was slow. "But this is the closest you've come to admitting that you do, too."

"Don't put words in my mouth."

The overhead light was suddenly blocked from their table. Pilar looked up, so oblivious to her surroundings that she hadn't noticed the man who had approached. The minute she recognized him, instinct pulled her hand away from Trace's.

"I hope I'm not intruding." The action didn't go unnoticed by Payne Forrestown, the corporate attorney for the Santee Line. There was a knowing light in his eyes as his glance went from one to the other. "I noticed you sitting here and thought I'd say hello."

"That was thoughtful of you, Payne." Trace

leaned back in his chair, aloofly studying the man. "I'd invite you to join us, but there's only room for two at our table." The message was clear that he wanted to keep it that way.

"That's quite all right. I have to be on my way," the lawyer assured him. "I had to spend the day in Jackson, so I need to get home. I only stopped in for coffee. It's quite a coincidence seeing the two of you in such an out-of-the-way place."

"It would seem so, yes," Pilar agreed, smiling a little too widely.

The waitress paused at their table. "Are you all ready to order dinner?"

"Yes, I think we are," Trace stated.

"I won't keep you," the attorney insisted and began to withdraw. "I'll be talking to you the latter part of this week, Trace."

Those few awkward moments after his departure were covered by the business of giving their meal order to the waitress. A silence reigned for several long minutes after that. Trace was leaning sideways in his chair, rubbing the back of his knuckles across his mouth in a thoughtful attitude. He barely looked at her at all. Finally his hand came down and he idly began to turn a knife over and over on the table, watching it. The air seemed heavy with unsettled currents.

"Would you like to explain again why you didn't want to go home and change clothes?" he challenged quietly.

"What?" She was confused as to the purpose of his question.

"Or maybe you'd like to explain why you wanted to eat here?" Trace suggested.

"It was close by. What is all this cross-examination?" Pilar attempted to laugh off the gravity in his look.

"Are you sure you didn't pick this restaurant because it was out of the way—and there was very little chance we'd be seen together by anyone we knew?" He made his meaning clearer, the hard angle of his jaw standing out.

"Possibly," she admitted, lowering her gaze to the tabletop.

"You were afraid people would start talking about us." It was close to an accusation. "Does the idea bother you?"

"Let's just say that I'd rather they didn't talk until there was something to talk about," Pilar replied defensively.

"Do you think there isn't already?" Trace seemed to mock her, and she flashed him an angry look. "Oh, Pilar." He shook his head in a kind of wry exasperation. "Do you think they haven't been talking before? Do you think no one has noticed the way I look at you—the way I have been looking at you for God knows how long? Don't you think they've guessed that I'd bed you the first chance I got?"

"But you didn't," she reminded him and ignored all the rest.

"Now who's bringing it up?" he countered roughly. "I had a feeling that night that I'd lose either way I went. Maybe I should have made love to you and let you hate me afterward. At least then it would have all been over and I wouldn't still be here, going through this hell."

"If you don't like it, you can always leave." Despite the shortness of her answer, she was holding her breath.

"I'm not ready to trade the hell I know for the hell I don't know," Trace replied and released a long breath. "Any hope you might have had about keeping this secret just went down the drain, you realize that? Men can be worse gossips than women. Payne is going to be sure that we've snuck out here because we have something to hide."

"I don't know why you're so upset about it," she said stiffly. "Other people's opinions have never mattered to you."

"That's true. I don't care what people say or think about me, but I can't be sure you won't let their talk influence you," was his response.

"I can make up my own mind." Pilar resented his implication. If she was so easily swayed by public opinion, she would never have married Elliot, a man over twice her own age, but she chose not to mention that to Trace.

"Well, you're damned slow about it," he muttered.

"That's your opinion."

"Pilar." An amused patience ran thickly through his voice, at odds with his previous curtness. "Don't you know why I'm suddenly in such a lousy mood? You aren't like me. The kind of talk that's likely to go around will probably hurt you, and there's nothing I can do to stop it."

"There's nothing either of us can do." But her resentment faded at his explanation. It was frustration he was voicing.

The waitress came with their salads, and there wasn't as much need for conversation to fill the silences. They talked infrequently through the meal and during the drive over the final miles to Natchez. Trace pulled the car up to the curb in front of an apartment building and switched off the motor.

"Is this where you live?" Pilar knew she was asking the obvious but it seemed necessary to hold at bay the sense of intimacy that accompanied the cessation of movement and the silence of the engine.

"I don't need much more than a place to sleep." Trace shrugged and half turned in the seat to rest his arm along the back near her head. "I don't suppose you'd come in for coffee."

"No."

"Pilar, I'm not a boy. I can't be satisfied with holding hands all night long." It was offered as an excuse as he cupped his hand to the back of her head and held it steady while he kissed her with slow, languid passion. "Neither of us is used to being satisfied with just that." He breathed the words into her mouth.

His hand stroked her face, making restless forays into her hair but avoiding any contact with her body. The ache was so quick to surface that Pilar felt wretched. It was such a crazy, mixed-up situation she'd made for herself—wanting him and not wanting to want him.

As he kissed her again, headlight beams raked the car and another vehicle pulled into the space in front of them. Trace drew reluctantly away from her and watched the couple climb out of the parked car to advance toward the apartment building. He waited until they were inside before he reached for the car door.

"I'll call you," he said.

Pilar nodded an acknowledgment, fully aware that his discretion was for her benefit. When he climbed out of the car, she slid into the driver's seat. It still held the warmth of his body. She watched his familiar long shape disappear into the building before she drove away.

There was a light on in the kitchen when she reached Dragon Walk. Instinct had made all the turns onto the roads that led home. Pilar remembered none of them.

"There you are," Cassie declared with a concerned sigh when Pilar walked through the back door. "I was just thinking about calling Digger to see if you'd had car problems or something. That auction surely didn't run this late."

"No. I stopped to eat on the way home. I—I'd better call Florence"—she changed what she was going to say—"and warn her to expect a delivery in the morning. I think I'll sleep in for a change."

Chapter Ten

$\mathcal{T}$oo much sleep had left her feeling drugged and dopey. The minute Pilar reached the kitchen, she walked straight for the coffeepot and poured herself a cup, hoping its caffeine would chase the dullness from her senses.

"Good morning to you, too." There was a snipping edge to Cassie's greeting as she stood at the sink, washing out one of her blouses by hand.

"Oh, good morning, Cassie. I'm sorry." Pilar apologized for not speaking and sagged into a kitchen chair. "I can't remember the last time I slept until noon. Now I wish I'd had you wake me up by, at least, ten. I feel awful."

There was no sympathy forthcoming from Cassie. She stood at the sink, shoulders rigidly squared as she rubbed vigorously at the delicate blouse material.

"Why didn't you mention to me that you were with Trace last night? And all afternoon, for that matter." Stiff displeasure was in every word as Cassie refused to turn around. "It isn't right that I'm the last one in the whole town to know."

"What?" Pilar frowned and mentally tried to shake off this slowness of her brain to function.

"I don't understand why you felt you couldn't tell me." Cassie candidly aired her hurt feelings. "It isn't as if I'd have told anyone else. At least I wouldn't have felt so foolish, standing there with my tongue in my mouth, unable to say a word because I didn't know what they were talking about when all those people called me this morning."

"Who called?" The hot liquid burned her throat when Pilar tried to sip her coffee.

"Oh, just the local busybodies who couldn't resist calling to see what I might let slip. They were in for a disappointment this time, because I didn't know what they were talking about." She squeezed the suds out of the blouse with a vengeance.

"I wasn't trying to hide it, Cassie." Pilar defended her previous night's silence on the subject. "I just didn't feel like talking about it last night. I didn't realize you'd find out before I had a chance to mention it."

Slightly mollified by the explanation, Cassie left her blouse to soak in some clear rinse water and poured herself a cup of coffee to join Pilar at the table. "If you knew these people, you'd know they could hardly wait for the chance to call and rub my nose in it. What's the point of gossip if it doesn't make someone uncomfortable? That's their reasoning."

"If they want to make a big deal out of the afternoon and evening I spent with Trace, there's nothing I can do about it." She folded her hands around the coffee cup and absently studied its mirror-smooth surface.

"They aren't the only ones who are making a big deal out of it." Cassie let her comment lie there without elaboration, knowing full well that she had Pilar's interest.

"What do you mean?"

"I mean Trace called the shop this morning, and became worried when he was told you weren't coming in. That's why he called here, to find out if something was wrong with you. I had a difficult time convincing him that you were merely sleeping late."

"Oh."

"Oh," Cassie repeated the noncommittal sound. "Is that all you have to say?"

Pilar lifted her gaze to the coffee-skinned woman, who was more like a roommate than anything else. They had shared so many happy things and sad things, confidences and confessions, yet in this one thing, she had never sought Cassie's counsel.

"You don't seem surprised by what people are suggesting," Pilar realized.

"Why should I be?" the woman reasoned with her usual calmness, which stood her in such good stead as a nurse. "I've known for a long time what kept Trace away from this house. And I hurt for him."

"You mean . . . you knew?"

"It wasn't what he wanted to feel. I could see him struggling inside with it sometimes." There was a slow sigh from her. "People can't always pick and choose who they want to love. It just happens to them." She studied Pilar for a short second. "And you . . . well, I would have been more worried about you if you hadn't found him attractive. You're a woman coming into the prime of her years, when your needs are stronger, and . . . you're alone. I know what that can be like. I went through it myself when my husband died."

"Afterward, did you meet someone like Trace?" Pilar wondered.

"Like Trace?" Cassie laughed shortly. "Now, I don't know what you mean by that. I guess I'd have to know how you feel about Trace before I could tell you."

"That's just it, Cassie." Pilar sighed and stared into her coffee, as if trying to see through its blackness. "I'm not sure how I feel toward him. It's hard to compare it with anything. It isn't at all like the love I felt for Elliot. There was so much happiness and tenderness with him . . . so much laughter and affection. With Trace, everything is so heated and intense. One minute it can be all friendly and natural, and the next there's a flashpoint and I get turned inside out." After hearing the words, Pilar smiled in faint wryness at herself. "The only time I can ever remember feeling anything close to this happened when I was fifteen and I had this wild crush on a local football star. One smile from him and I could float on a cloud for a week, and be equally devastated if he failed to acknowledge me when we passed in the school halls." She looked at her friend. "What do you think?"

"Well, I think . . ." Cassie paused to stand up and walk back to the sink to finish rinsing her blouse. ". . . some things in your life have happened backward."

"What do you mean?" Pilar found that to be a curious statement. She straightened from the chair and wandered to the sink.

"Usually when you're young, you find a passionate kind of love that follows no particular rhyme or reason. Then when you get older, you want something warm and loving. You skipped the first and went straight to the second when you married Elliot," she explained. "So you see, there wasn't anyone like Trace for me, because my Oggie was Trace."

"I see." Pilar sipped slowly at her coffee to give herself time to think. "Passion usually burns itself out, though." She spoke aloud the doubts that assailed her. "When it's dead, there usually isn't anything left."

"Passion eventually burns itself up," Cassie agreed. "But passionate love is another thing entirely. Some of us are lucky enough to find it, others find an equally satisfying substitute, and the rest make do. Passionate love means passionate caring. He's got to mean something more than just a man you want to sleep in your bed. How do you describe an emotion that doesn't need words?" She shook her head, unable to come up with a way. "Desire is a part of it, but it only makes the caring richer."

"Everything is so tangled up inside me that I don't know anything, Cassie. I like him. I'm even beginning to understand him." She laughed softly at that. "But . . . I question whether the desire can last. I don't trust my own emotions."

"For your own sake, you need to decide," Cassie advised. "Sometimes making no decision is worse than making the wrong one."

"I love it when you give me one of those adages of yours," Pilar chided affectionately. "They sound so wise and they're so impossible to carry out." She finished her coffee and set the empty cup on the drainboard. "I'd better get to the shop before Florence decides that I'm not coming in at all today."

Pilar was in the rear storeroom of the antique shop, checking over the items she'd purchased the day before at the auction and making sure none had been damaged in transport. Florence Barslow was on her way out the rear door to take her noon break, a little late in the day. The bell above the shop door jangled the entrance of a customer.

"Would you want me to wait on them while you finish up?" Florence volunteered.

"No, I'll get it. You run along." Pilar set her notes aside and stepped over the pile of discarded newspaper and tissue-packing to cross the storeroom to the retail section of the shop.

When Trace saw her, he paused in midstride, then came to the counter. "So you finally made it to work. I missed you at the house. I called a few minutes ago and Cassie said you'd left to come here."

"Was there something urgent?" There was a quicksilver racing along her nerve ends.

"Foolish question," he mocked dryly. "Where you're concerned, my needs are always urgent."

Deciding it was better if she didn't reply to that, she chose to comment on something else. "Are you playing hookey again today?" She noticed the way the blue-gray suit fit him, comfortably molding the tapering width of his body.

"No. I just came by for two reasons," he said.

"And they are?" she prompted.

"I wondered if you were still planning to go to New Orleans next week." The counter was between them. Trace picked up a glass paperweight and leaned a hip against the counter while he examined the blown crystal glass.

"Yes, I am."

"I believe I mentioned to you that our new towboat was due to come out of the boatyards about that same time." He set the paperweight onto the counter again. "The date happens to coincide with your trip. It seemed appropriate to me that you should be on hand to christen the newest member of the Santee river fleet when it's launched for the first time."

"Do you mean . . . with champagne?" The idea intrigued her.

"How's your swinging arm?" Trace inquired. "You have to hit that champagne bottle across the bow in just the right spot to break it."

"It should be fun." She warmed to the plan.

"Come on." He caught her hand and pulled her around the counter. Before she could guess his intentions, he had her standing with her back to him and his arms were guiding her into a swinging position. "We'll practice a few times." But he was nuzzling her hair, working his way through its silken mass to her ear.

"Trace, don't." His breath stirred little shivers to race over her skin. She brought her arms down, but his hands followed them and folded her arms across her middle to draw her backward into his long length. "There are people outside. They can see us through the window."

"So? Let them." But he made no attempt to check her escape when she moved shakily out of his arms.

"This is a place of business," she retorted impatiently. "How would you like it if I walked into your office while you were working and proceeded to crawl onto your lap?" The instant she saw the wicked gleam in his eyes, Pilar immediately retracted her question. "Don't bother to answer that."

"So we're in public, hmm? And it's back to hand holding." He reached for her hand and carried it to his mouth, where he kissed her fingertips with consummate ease. She snatched her hand away before she began to enjoy the sensation too much.

"Is this why you came here? Just to mock me?" As she turned away she laughed in irony. "And to think that just this morning I was saying to Cassie that I thought I was beginning to understand you."

"Did you? What else did you tell her about me?" he asked.

"It's none of your business." She tried not to let that huskily seductive pitch of his voice insinuate itself into her confidence.

"If I was the subject being discussed, whose business would it be if it isn't mine?" Trace chided her mockingly. "Maybe I'll have to stop by the house and talk to Cassie. It's pretty hard for her to keep anything from me."

"There's nothing she can tell you that you don't already know." Pilar didn't doubt that he had the wiles to maneuver Cassie into disclosing their conversation without realizing she had.

"Which is?" He was doing it to her.

"That everything is a tangled mess."

"We'll never straighten it out if we don't spend time together," he responded seriously.

"I'm well aware of your idea of time together."

"Are you?" he countered. "My idea is that we go to New Orleans together—get away by ourselves where the wrong noses won't keep sticking themselves into our business and you won't have to worry about who's watching."

"Alone? With you? No." That was asking for trouble.

"I guessed you'd say that, so I have an alternative," Trace replied. "The new towboat will go out on a shakedown cruise after it's launched. We can ride on it as far as Natchez, which is somewhere around a two-day trip, depending on the conditions. Have you ever been on the river?"

"Only in pleasure craft," she admitted.

"Then you'll have a chance to learn first-hand what the business is all about. As part owner of the company, it's something you should know." The rough contours of his lean features showed a dry pleasure at how nicely the reason dovetailed into his plans for spending time together. "We'll drive up on Monday. There's no need for you to take your car or it will wind up stranded in New Orleans."

"But I'll need transportation once I'm there so I can make my calls on the various antique shops." That was the only inconvenience Pilar foresaw.

"We'll arrange for you to have the loan of

someone's car." Trace solved it without hesitation and moved toward her. "That's all settled. Now what about the weekend?"

"I'll be attending auctions both days," Pilar explained as he reached up to smooth the collar of her blouse.

Lightly curling his fingers under the lapels, he followed them down to the first button, nestled at the top of her cleavage. Her flesh tingled in vague excitement where the backs of his hands brushed the curves of her breasts.

"That takes care of the days," he murmured. "What about the nights?"

Struggling to keep her composure from being affected by his disturbing touch, Pilar attempted to hold the gaze of his velvety gray eyes. "I think we need a cooling-off period."

"Cooling off." He chuckled softly in his throat and edged closer to add the persuasions of his body to the faint caress of his hands. "I haven't even gotten warmed up yet."

"All right, maybe you don't, but I need time to sort things out," she insisted, rawly conscious of the slight pressure of his thighs against hers. "Sometimes I don't even like you." Mostly because he knew just how to get to her and upset the comfortable balance of her life.

"You don't like me?" He ran a finger down the pulsing vein in her neck. "Or is it that you don't like what I do to you?"

"I don't trust it," she answered truthfully.

"There has to be more than just this, otherwise—"

"Otherwise we can roll in the sack a few times and get it out of our system," Trace inserted his suggestion. "It's not a bad idea and it just might answer some things for you."

"I am not naive." She was impatient with him, mostly because the suggestion was so damned tempting regardless of her ability to dismiss his rationale. "Having sex with a man is no way to judge how much you like him. And if you don't mind, I'd like to find that out before I get in bed with him."

"Sometimes it's hard to separate the two," he murmured while his restless hands idly caressed her face, neck, and shoulders to constantly remind her that it wouldn't take much provocation on her part to turn this closeness into an embrace.

The clapper rattled against the sides of the bell to signal the opening of the shop door. Sidestepping quickly, Pilar swung out from behind Trace to greet the incoming customer. It was her own discomfort and shakey limbs that put the high color in her cheeks.

"Oh, hello, Pilar." Except for a faintly curious glance, Sybil Anderson barely took any notice of Trace when she entered the shop. "Is Florence here? She called me this morning to say you had come across an unusually shaped bowl that might be a nice addition to my collection of Depression glass."

"Florence is out to lunch but I know the piece she means," Pilar assured her. "It's still in the storeroom. We haven't brought it out yet. If you'll wait here, I'll get it for you."

"Of course."

Trace's voice checked her movement to the rear of the shop. "It's time I was getting back to the office. We'll get an early start Monday morning, probably around six. And be sure to pack some everyday clothes for the trip back. You might want to bring a light jacket. Sometimes it gets cool on the river at night."

"I . . . I will." She nodded, aware of the woman's sharpening curiosity. The bell jangled behind Trace as he walked out of the shop onto the street.

"Evidently you and Trace are planning a trip somewhere," Sybil Anderson concluded, barely containing her desire to know all the details.

"Yes. We're going to New Orleans on Monday." Pilar tried to sound very matter-of-fact about it. "The Santee Line is launching a new boat on Tuesday. Trace thought I might enjoy making its inaugural trip upstream. It should be an interesting experience."

"Yes . . . I guess it would." She sounded disappointed.

The early-morning sunlight had dispelled the white mists that had been drifting close to the ground under the moss-draped oaks. The softness of that early light was gentle on everything it touched, toning down harsh colors and rounding rough edges. Pilar followed Trace out of the rear door of Dragon Walk, her weekender bag in his hand. Cassie paused in the doorway.

"Now, you drive carefully," she admonished.

"Now, Cassie, whenever have I ever taken chances?" Trace mockingly chided her words of caution.

"Everytime you do anything," she retorted.

Trace merely laughed and continued toward the car, parked in the rear driveway. Pilar had barely glanced at it. But as they approached it she happened to notice someone sitting in the rear seat.

"You never mentioned that someone would be riding with us," she murmured in a low voice so her comment wouldn't carry through the open car window.

"Didn't I?" He unlocked the trunk and stowed her suitcase inside. "Mike's coming to handle all the paperwork and drive my car back. I thought you'd be pleased to have a chaperon on the long drive to New Orleans." He was mocking her. "You made it very definite that you didn't want to be alone with me."

"I don't mind a bit." Pilar shrugged despite the niggling sense of disappointment. "It was just a surprise, that's all."

Although Trace installed her in the front passenger seat next to him, she took very little part in the conversation that went on, letting the business talk swirl around her. Most of the time she looked out the window to avoid staring at Trace.

The warm and humid summer climate of the South made everything lush and green. Here and there along the highway there were glimpses of old homes, examples of the gracious architecture that had grown out of more languorous times. There were signs of poverty, too, but the benign surroundings seemed to remove some of the grimness that was usually associated with it in other parts of the country.

"Are we boring you, Pilar?" Trace inquired when it had been a long time since she had contributed anything to the conversation.

"No." She turned and experienced the warm caress of his gaze traveling over her. "I was just enjoying the scenery."

"It can be very stimulating at times." His mouth twitched in a half smile, and his look turned her into the subject of his comment instead of the countryside they were passing.

She breathed in deeply, unable to respond with Mike listening from his rear seat post, and turned to gaze out the window again. Yet there was an awareness of the warm pleasure that licked along her nerve ends at the subtle and suggestive compliment.

When they reached New Orleans, Trace drove straight to the hotel in the French Quarter where they'd be spending the night. "As Mike could tell you," he said as the doorman approached to assist them from the car and see to their luggage, "normally when we come to the city on business, our accommodations aren't this lavish. Since you're with us, and this trip is something of an occasion, it seemed the perfect excuse to treat ourselves to some luxury."

"It wasn't necessary on my account." She didn't want him to think she expected any special treatment.

"Don't say that," Mike Barnes protested in mock seriousness. "Ever since Trace mentioned you were coming to attend the launching, I've done my best to convince him it wouldn't be right for a lady to stay in that fleabag hotel near the terminal office."

"It isn't that bad," Trace countered and stepped out of the car so the parking valet could put it in the hotel garage.

"Maybe not, but this is better," Mike announced, running an appreciative eye over the impressive hotel entrance.

"In that case, Mike, this is exactly where I wanted to stay." Pilar smiled, supporting his case.

As the driver slid behind the wheel, Trace slipped him a tip. "We'll be needing the car in about an hour. Mrs. Santee will be picking it up." He indicated Pilar with a nod of his head, then joined her on the front walk. "You can use my car to make your calls. Fitzroy is picking up Mike and me and driving us to our local office."

His guiding hand was spread along the back of her waist as Trace escorted her inside the hotel. Warmth radiated from the contact, a hint of possession in the gesture that was oddly pleasing to Pilar. The passing glances they attracted gave her a feeling of pride at being with him. As well dressed as any man in the lobby, Trace had rough, manly airs about him; he was lean and raw, experienced in the ways of men—and women—and possessed with a keen intelligence that revealed itself in the alertness of his unusual gray eyes. It was slightly funny that she had to see him outside normal surroundings before she noticed any of that.

At the reception desk Pilar stepped to one side while Trace checked on their reservations. The clerk punched the information into the computer and waited for the readout on the screen.

"Mr. Santee," he confirmed, then glanced at Pilar. "And you are Mrs. Santee?"

"Yes." She nodded.

"And another gentleman by the name of Mr. Barnes," the clerk added. "Is that all in your party, Mr. Santee?" he inquired and pushed the sequence of characters to print out a computerized form.

"That's correct."

"Just sign here, Mr. Santee." The clerk indicated the signature blank on the form, handed him a pen, then tore off a perforated end after Trace had signed it and gave it to him. "Just give this to the bellboy. He'll get your key and take you and your wife to your room."

There was a slight pause during which Trace slid an amused look at Pilar. "You have Mrs. Santee and myself in the same room."

A vaguely bewildered expression crossed the clerk's face. "Yes, sir."

"It's not that I have any objections to the arrangements." A smile kept playing with the corners of his mouth, and Pilar shared his secret amusement even though her senses were tingling with the possibility of sharing a room with him. "But I believe when the reservations were made, a separate room was requested for Mrs. Santee. You see, she isn't my wife, although I don't deny the idea does have some appeal."

The young clerk became slightly flustered. "I beg your pardon," he apologized anxiously and quickly punched up the computer readout again. "You're right. It was my mistake. Another room has been assigned to Mrs. Santee."

As soon as that mix-up was straightened out, Trace handed her the separate slip to give to the bellboy. "More's the pity," he murmured in a low voice.

"I was sure that was what you were thinking," she replied in an equally soft tone.

After Mike had registered, the bellboy with their luggage passed out their respective keys and rode with them on the elevator to their assigned floor. Pilar was shown to her room first.

Left alone when the others were taken to their quarters, she took a few minutes to unpack some things she didn't want wrinkled. As she finished there was a knock at her door.

"Who is it?"

"Trace."

After slipping the chain free of its catch, Pilar opened the door and Trace stepped inside. "Mike and I are meeting Fitzroy downstairs in the lobby, so I won't see you until tonight."

"What time will we be having dinner?" She had a strange feeling all this talk was superfluous.

"Eight, I suppose. The manager of this office will be joining us." His mouth crooked at a rueful angle. "I told you it would all be very proper, didn't I?"

"You did."

His hand reached out and pushed the door closed behind him before he took a step toward her and gathered her up into the tight circle he made with his arms and his body. She had already lifted her head to meet his oncoming mouth. It rolled onto her lips, all raw and hungry. It seemed to consume her with a surging rush of fierce need that soon ignited an answering ache.

But Trace pulled away before she was satisfied and buried his face in the side of her hair near an ear. He was breathing hard, the hot rush of moist air igniting her skin and sending fevered chills over her nerve ends.

"I needed that," he muttered thickly. "After being so close to you all that way in the car, I thought I'd go as mad as Tantalus. I wonder how much it would cost me to bribe the clerk into giving me a key to your room so I could slip in here in the middle of the night—"

"Trace—" She was caught halfway between excitement and trepidation.

"Don't worry. I won't." There was an impatient edge in his voice as his hands tightened on her shoulders to set her away from him. "If I thought I had a single chance in hell of accomplishing something, I'd do it. It's for damned sure, I'm not looking forward to looking at you all evening, not with everyone else at our table."

With a new perspective on the control he was exercising over his wants and the strain it was putting on him, Pilar felt an inexplicable need to test this newly discovered power she had over him.

"It could be worse," she warned with faint mockery. "You could be here and I could be in Natchez."

"Some consolation," he mocked. "At least tomorrow I'll have you all to myself on that boat."

"Doesn't the boat have a crew?" She playfully tilted her head to the side, half taunting him.

"Yes, but they'll be busy. And if they're not,

I'll see to it that something is found for them to do," Trace retorted. "Not that it matters. They're rivermen. They aren't going to talk about the private affairs of one of their own." He planted a hard kiss on her lips. "I'd better go. Mike's waiting."

Chapter Eleven

𝒯he sun made a bright glare on the muddy Mississippi water when they arrived at dock-side the next morning. More than a dozen people were already on hand for the launching of the new towboat, fully equipped with all the latest navigation and communications devices. There was a chorus of greetings as they approached the group. It was a few minutes before the glad-handing was over and Trace took the opportunity to introduce the men to Pilar.

"I think you know Sam, Frank, and Adam from our New Orleans terminal." The three men nodded to Pilar when Trace pointed them out to her. "And this man"—he slapped the shoulder of a slight-built man, about Trace's age, wearing a white shirt, a navy blue waist-jacket, and a captain's hat—"is Dan Morgan. He'll be piloting the *Santee Lady* when she puts out."

"How do you do," Pilar greeted him as he briefly lifted his hat to her.

"What Trace failed to tell you," Morgan said, "is that I was second pilot under him for a long time. We plied these waters many a time together. It'll be like old times to have him back on board when we make this trial run." Then, as if remembering his manners, he added, "It'll be a pleasure to have you with us, too."

"Thank you. I'm looking forward to it." It had the sound of an adventure about it, something totally new and out of the ordinary. An earlier remark by Trace had caught her interest, and she went back to it before he could complete the introductions. "What did you say the name of the boat is going to be?"

"The *Santee Lady*." Behind the lazy look he gave her, there was something warm and suggestive. "It seemed fitting to name her after one of the owners of the company." He held her gaze for an instant longer, then made an obvious effort to break away from it. "This is Pete Turner, the engineer. And the deckhands for this trip—" Four men were standing in a loose row and he went down them, pointing them out as he gave her their names. "Joe Allen, Billy Bob Davis, Rick Connors, and Tucker Smith. And last but not least, the most important member of the crew, Woody Evers, the cook."

"Hello." She addressed her response to all of them.

Evers removed the cigar from his mouth long enough to say, "Pleased to meet you," then clamped it between his lips again.

"Evers' reputation as a cook is known up and down the river," Trace explained with a sly smile. "Most people don't know why his food always tastes so different. But his secret ingredient is that cigar that's always hanging out of his mouth. The smoke flavors everything he fixes."

The cigar was obviously an inhouse joke, since the others laughed heartily at Trace's jibing remarks and gave the cook a rough time about it. The interplay permitted Pilar a glimpse of the rough-and-tumble life Trace had once led.

Before the round of introductions was completed, she had met representatives from the boat builder as well as two officers from the Coast Guard. A lot of general conversations went back and forth, some idle bantering and speculation about the new towboat.

"Shall we get on with the ceremony?" Trace suggested and half turned. "Mike? You brought along the requisite bottle of champagne, didn't you?"

"Got it right here." He produced the bottle with a ribboned bow around its neck and handed it to Pilar.

"Come on." Trace led her to the freshly painted bow of the towboat where it sat on a ramp to the water. "Do you see this area right here?" He showed her a section of the angled edge of the bow. "Take the bottle in both hands and swing it just as hard as you can and aim it for this spot. Okay?"

"Okay." She nodded.

"Everybody stand back," Trace advised as he moved away from her. "I don't know what she's going to hit. If she had her choice, it'd probably be me."

There was a certain awkwardness to the moment as Pilar gripped the neck of the bottle as if it were a baseball bat and kept her eye on the spot Trace had indicated.

"Remember those newsreels they used to show?" Evers was saying in the background. "I remember seeing one this one time where some woman kept trying to bust a bottle of champagne over the bow of this brand new Navy ship. She never did do it."

"Thanks for the encouragement," Pilar inserted dryly.

She drew the bottle back, then took aim and swung as hard as she could. She felt the jolt of the bottle hitting the bow and flinched in anticipation of the splintering crash that followed and the spray of champagne. There was a burst of cheers—more from surprise than anything else, she suspected. She stepped away from the bow, shaking the wetness of champagne from her hands while she continued to hold the ribboned neck of the bottle.

"You did it!" Trace's arm hugged her by the

shoulders while his broad, laughing smile beamed at her with pride. "The first time, too."

Someone was already picking up the larger, broken chunks of glass as Trace led her back to join the others at the top of the ramp.

"Didn't you think I could?" she challenged him and offered him the broken bottle neck as proof.

"I'm beginning to think you can do everything except make up your mind," he declared, but in a low voice, meant for her hearing alone.

A second later Pilar was caught up in the rush of voices congratulating her. Someone popped the cork of a chilled bottle of champagne and paper cups of it were passed around for the toasting as the lines securing and steadying the towboat eased it gently into the water.

An hour later the Coast Guard had completed its final inspection of the craft and the towboat was chugging out of the boatyard area. The New Orleans harbor was busy, tugs and towboats moving steadily up-and-downstream, freighters and cargo ships tied up to wharfs.

Beyond the high levees that kept the Mississippi River within its banks was the city of New Orleans, its streets below the river's waterline. Leaning forward, Pilar rested her forearms on the deck railing outside the pilothouse, feeling a part of all this subtle excitement.

"Wait until you see how she handles, Trace," Dan Morgan said from inside the house. "She likes a lover's touch. No rough stuff for this lady."

"Is that right?" The idle response came from a point very close to her. Pilar glanced over her shoulder to discover that Trace was studying her intently. "Is that where I made my mistake with you?" he murmured to her.

She looked to the front again, her side vision noting his approach to stand beside her at the railing. "You like saying things that are slightly unnerving to me, don't you?" she accused, conscious of how erratic her pulse had become at his suggestive comment.

"Not nearly as much as I like doing things that slightly unnerve you," he replied.

"You're doing it again," Pilar said.

"All right then, no more words," he said. "Why don't I take you below and show you which cabin will be yours? You'd probably like to change clothes."

"Yes, I would," she agreed, having already discovered that her leather-soled shoes were not the best choice.

When she stepped over the raised threshold into the cabin, Pilar discovered that it was larger than she had guessed it would be. Everything was brand-new and gleaming. It was all so compact and efficient, yet so much roomier than she had expected.

"This is nice," she said to Trace with a degree of surprise when he followed her into the cabin.

"It's the captain's quarters. Morgan willingly gave it up one night for you," he said as he wandered into the cabin, idly looking around. "It's a home away from home. Or in some instances, this is home and the house on land is the second home. This is where they live and they vacation somewhere else."

"Was a place like this home for you?" Pilar heard the undertones of nostalgia in his voice and wondered about this side of his life. She halted by the bunk and sat down.

"Yes." He wandered over and sat down next to her. "It should be comfortable."

Pilar stood up and moved away from the bed before the thoughts that were in his mind became actions. "I'm sure it will be very comfortable."

Turning his body, he stretched out on the bed and cradled his hands under his head. "This bed is going to be the envy of every riverman up and down the way. Morgan's lucky."

"Why?" Although she sensed she was walking into something, she had to ask.

"Because you're going to sleep in this bed tonight. A man's imagination can keep that dream alive every time he crawls into this bunk and thinks of you in it."

"Did you ever have a woman aboard?" She supposed it was natural curiosity that prompted her to inquire about his previous affairs. Not for a minute did she believe there hadn't been any before her.

"I've entertained women in my cabin before," he admitted. "But I don't want to talk about them. I want to talk about you."

"And I want to change clothes." Pilar reminded him of the reason he had ostensibly shown her the location of the cabin. She wasn't ready for the discussion to become personal.

"Go ahead and change." He settled more comfortably into the bunk.

"Trace, I'm not going to stand here and strip for your benefit," she advised him with a small laugh.

"Come here a minute," he urged and sat up on one elbow.

Hesitantly Pilar moved to the edge of the bunk. "What do you want?"

"You." He caught her hand and pulled her onto the mattress, turning her with his hands to lay her down beside him. "All this talk and where's it getting us? Not where either of us want to be, which is right here."

His hand glided across her stomach and covered a round breast. There was no sound she could utter, nothing she could say as he lowered himself toward her. His kiss was long and slow, plunging deep to curl her toes with sensation. He hooked a leg between hers as his body became pleasantly heavy on her. Every inch of her face was covered by his seeking mouth, down her lips to the hollow at her throat.

"It's no good, Pilar." It was a thickly murmured comment, half muffled by her skin. "I love you too much. I've got to know."

"Don't ask me now," she protested on an aching whisper. "I'd say anything just because I love what you're doing to me. It isn't fair to tell you that."

With a groan he turned his head aside. "When will it be fair?" he demanded.

His hands ceased their stroking arousal, and some of her sanity seemed to return. She twisted from beneath him and swung out of the bunk. Her blouse was half unbuttoned and she was still quaking inside.

"I'm sorry, Trace, but I don't know," she insisted and felt that awful twist of agony when she heard him angrily rise from the bed.

"I don't know how much more of this I can take," he muttered.

"Neither do I," Pilar retorted. "And I wish you'd stop making me feel like some cheap tease who gets her kicks out of doing this to a man."

"You'd better change." He breathed out heavily, as if trying to release some of that taut emotion. "I'll see you topside."

It was several minutes after Trace had left the cabin before Pilar even bothered to open her suitcase to take out the jeans and sleeveless white blouse she'd brought along. When she had changed her clothes, she sat on a chair to tie on a pair of rubber-soled deck shoes.

There was suddenly a hard jolt as if they'd run into something. Alarmed, she quickly finished tying her shoes and hurried to the door.

Vaguely she remembered the varying pitches of the engine, but she had merely assumed they were testing something.

She practically flew through the companionway and up the ladders to the pilothouse, where Trace had said he was going. She stopped in the open doorway, clutching the sides, slightly out of breath.

"What happened?" She was panting as she looked past the two men in the pilothouse at an obscured view of a wharf.

"Nothing." Trace appeared calm and completely unperturbed. "Why?"

"I thought . . . didn't we run into something?" She ducked her head back outside to look to the bow.

"No," he replied.

"Well, we did bump the barges a bit. Maybe that's what she felt," Dan Morgan suggested.

"Oh." Feeling a little sheepish, Pilar backed out of the pilothouse and stuck her hands in the hip pockets of her jeans as she wandered forward.

If she had taken the time to look, she realized she would have seen there wasn't any trouble. From her high vantage point, she could see the deckhands working below. They seemed to be securing a set of four barges, tied abreast, to the towboat. Pilar frowned, a little confused. When she heard Trace step onto the deck behind her, she turned.

"What are they doing?" she asked.

He came to the railing beside her and looked

down expectantly, then slid her a puzzled glance. "What do you mean? They're making the barges fast."

"But—" She shrugged. "I thought this was going to be a trial run just to test it out. You're going to push barges, too?"

"Only four. We aren't taking a full complement. We want enough to put some strain on the engines and check how they function," he explained with an indulgent look, then turned back to watch the working men. His expression sobered slightly. "From the looks of that river, it's going to do some testing of its own."

Earlier Pilar had been more interested in what was going on around her than the muddy water rolling around the boat. But his comment drew her attention to the foamy brown water, churning and boiling below her. It was swollen, with odd bits of debris and broken branches tossed and sucked under by its angry current.

"It's high, isn't it?" she realized.

"They've been having a lot of heavy rains up north," he stated. "The runoff has swollen the Mississippi, which makes for turbulent water and stronger, fast-running currents. The gal's gonna be tested going upstream against this," Trace concluded, referring to the boat.

"Do you think she'll make it?"

Trace looked at her. "I'm betting on it." Everything with him seemed to have a double meaning.

"I think Cassie's right—you like taking chances," she replied and lowered her gaze to the swollen river.

"The Mississippi is an amazing thing when you think about it," he said, changing the subject.

"Why is that?"

"It drains nearly half the total area of the United States. The Indians named it right when they called it the Father of Waters," he said idly. "That water down there—some of it probably dripped off a house in Pennsylvania and flowed into the Ohio, or it came from Wyoming and Montana down the Yellowstone and into the Mississippi by way of the Missouri. The muddy Missouri—too thick to drink and too thin to plow. The Tennessee drains into it, reaching all the way back to North Carolina, and the Platte from Colorado. Not to mention all that Texas rain that dumps into the Mississippi where the Red River flows into it above Baton Rouge. And that's just the big rivers. That doesn't count all the smaller tributaries and streams."

"It almost sounds like a geography lesson." She laughed.

"I guess it does," he agreed with a slow smile, then pushed away from the rail. "I think I'll go check to see how much longer we'll be here. You're free to wander around anyplace."

For the time being, Pilar stayed at her vantage point to observe the proceedings and left the exploring for another time. She listened to the orders shouted and the acknowledgments made in answering yells.

It didn't seem to take long, and the towboat was maneuvering into the channel, pushing the heavily loaded barges ahead of it. The deck vibrated with the hard throb of the engines. Atop the pilothouse the radar disc began to make its slow, never-ending circle.

A scorching sun was high overhead, sending Pilar in search of the shady side to escape its direct heat. As they chugged steadily upstream, the signs of the city gradually faded from view and Pilar saw levee banks and the cotton, cane, and rice fields beyond.

"Hey, Pilar!" a voice shouted to her. She looked over the railing to see Trace standing on the lower deck, his hand cupped to his mouth. "Lunch's ready! Are you hungry?"

"Yes!" She nodded emphatically to be sure he understood and hurried down the ladder to join him.

The meal was served in a common room off the galley. Between meals it was a gathering place to play cards or watch television or talk. At this mealtime it was filled with hungry men and one woman, Pilar.

After Trace's comment about the cook's flavoring his dishes with cigar smoke, he took a lot of ribbing from the crew. It was a hearty meal, the simple meat, potato, and vegetable kind with a fruit pie for dessert.

When she was finished, Pilar carried her dirty dishes into the galley like all the others had. Evers was grumbling sourly under his breath at the sink, the cigar wigwagging from his mouth.

"Don't pay any attention to them, Mr. Evers," Pilar said quietly as she set her dishes with the rest. "The food was very good and none of it tasted of cigar." But she suspected it wouldn't be long before the galley stank with its smoke.

"They gotta have somethin' to complain about, ma'am. If it ain't me and my cookin', it'll be somethin' else." He shrugged his disinterest in their jibes at him, but the cigar settled into one place in his mouth, proving to Pilar that her compliment had slightly mollified his ego.

When she returned to the common room, Trace was standing. He stretched taller, his flexing shoulders pulling the shirt tautly across his chest as he rubbed a hand absently across his stomach. He smiled faintly at her.

"Ready to go for a walk?"

"After that meal I need it," she agreed and moved in front of him to step through the doorway first.

"Well, what do you think of it so far?" He wrapped an arm around her waist, keeping her close despite the sultry blast of outside heat.

"Everything's so new to me. I feel like a child, always wanting to ask 'What's that?'" She laughed.

"Such as?" Trace wanted to know.

"Such as . . ." Pausing, Pilar looked around

and spied one of the deckhands heading for the steps by the tall bumpers that led down to the barges. "What's he doing?"

"I imagine he's going to check the cables and make sure they're all tight. They tend to work loose, especially in turbulent currents like this." The response was barely given before a black look spread across his features. Pilar suddenly felt herself being shoved aside as Trace pushed by her. "Stay here," he ordered and appeared to forget her instantly. "Tucker!" he shouted to the deckhand. "Where the hell do you think you're going?"

The man stopped and looked at him blankly, a half-smoked cigarette drooping from one side of his mouth. In two strides Trace was there and snatching the cigarette from his mouth to throw it into the river.

"Dammit all, Tucker! You know better!" he snapped. "Have you forgotten we're carrying sulfur in the holds of those barges? It's carelessness that gets people killed."

"Sorry, I . . . forgot." The man went almost white.

"See that you don't forget again," Trace ordered. "And when you've checked those lines, make sure 'No Smoking' signs get posted."

There was still a dark scowl on his face when he returned to Pilar. She didn't have to ask what that was all about, since it was impossible not to overhear.

"The barges are loaded with sulfur? Is that explosive?" she asked curiously.

His glance was brief and his response was briefer. "It's what they use on match heads." No further explanation was required. "Come on." That displeasure lingered in his eyes despite his attempt to push it aside. "I'll show you around the *Lady*."

"All right." Pilar preferred a guided tour to exploring on her own.

He took her through the crew's quarters, then below to the engine room, where the whining throb of the engines was so loud that he had to shout to make himself heard. Since this was a shakedown trip, a lot of checks were being made of the systems. Trace took time to speak with the engineer before escorting Pilar out of the room.

From the engine room they went topside to the pilothouse. A breeze, at least, moved the air around even though the sun kept it sticky and hot. Trace relieved Morgan at the wheel, then explained all the sophisticated equipment to her. When they came to a straight stretch of river, he let her steer, with some instructions and occasional assistance.

When he came up behind her and nibbled on her neck, Pilar wasn't surprised. Sooner or later she had expected him to take advantage of the fact that she had both hands on the wheel.

"Pay attention to where you're going," he warned when she tried to twist away from him. "You have to stay inside the channel markers unless you want to run us aground."

"Isn't there some law against interfering

with the pilot?" She protested and tried to shrug a shoulder into her neck to stop that exciting nibbling of her skin.

"Probably," he agreed and lifted his head, but he continued to stand directly behind her, his hands rubbing her with disturbing interest.

Now that he had stopped that sensual nibbling, Pilar leaned back against him, contentment sighing through her at the hard, solid warmth of his body, whipped lean and rugged. "I can't remember the last time I enjoyed myself so much," she declared.

"Then don't try," Trace replied.

It was an idyllic afternoon she spent with him. Sometimes it was fun and playful; other times it was simply quiet and companionable, talking about little things or events in their respective lives or watching the wildlife along the banks.

Sundown brought a lowering of temperature, aided by the water-cooled breeze coming off the river. Trace's arm was draped around her shoulders as they took a late-night stroll, leaving behind the lighted decks of the towboat to venture onto the shadowed barges. The vibrating throb of the powerful engines ceased to dominate the night and faded into the background, the breeze blowing the sound away from them.

When they reached the bow of the lead barge on the port side, they paused to look out into the black silhouettes of the night and listen to the rush of water against the sides. It was like being totally alone, only the two of them in the world. The slight pressure of his arm urged her downward as Trace lowered himself onto the barge deck and leaned against an idle ratchet. Pilar readily joined him, nestling herself in the crook of his arm and resting her head against his shoulder.

A fat, lopsided moon grinned down from a night sky jam-packed with stars. The midnight blackness was virtually littered with the tinsel-bright glitter of them. There was a magic about the night that vaguely dazzled her.

"I've never seen so many stars," she murmured.

"Beautiful, isn't it?" he agreed.

Turning her head against his shoulder, Pilar gazed up at him. "You miss this, don't you?" She noticed the ease in his features.

Here there were no walls and no desks to confine him, no expensive silk tie around his neck or tailored suit jacket constricting his shoulders. He had on a pair of worn jeans and a dark windbreaker over a plain cotton shirt, unbuttoned at the throat, and that slightly battered captain's hat was on his head. That had been his attire since they'd come aboard.

"Yes," Trace admitted. "I'm not sure I make a good corporate executive, but I enjoy the challenge of running things even if I can't stand all the paperwork and meetings. Whenever I get the urge to chuck it all, I spend a couple of days on the river and come back." One corner of his mouth lifted in the suggestion of a smile as his lazy glance roamed her upturned face. "A couple of times I've been tempted to buy myself a boat and run the company from it."

"Would that make you happy?" she wondered, because there was a lurking quality of sadness about him despite the occasional bravado.

"Pilar." He breathed heavily with patient exasperation. "How many times do I have to tell you—you would make me happy."

This sudden turn of the conversation, where she became the subject matter, made her uneasy. It was that subtle pressuring again, trying to force a decision from her. She lowered her chin to break away from his gaze and looked at the swallowing blackness of the river.

"Maybe I haven't been patient, but you've lived inside me a long time. It's already to the point where there's no getting over you." His warm lips nuzzled her temple, the need in his voice closing her eyes and shutting off her breath. "After waiting so long, I thought I could wait another day, another week or month, if that's what it would take. But it isn't working out that way. I can't hold you and kiss you without wanting all of you. I want to read the end of the book, Pilar, and find out if they lived happily ever after."

"Trace, you're asking the impossible," she protested achingly.

"Am I?" He cupped her cheek in his hand and turned her face up. "All I know is the longer I have to wait, the worse the odds get. As corny as it sounds, Natchez isn't big enough for the both of us. If you haven't decided yet, then your answer is going to be no. If that's the way it's going to be, then you've seen the last of me. If it's over with us, the best thing is to end it all—move the company, lock, stock, and barrel, to another port and never come near you again." He watched her lips, the strain showing as he resisted their closeness. "We should reach Natchez tomorrow afternoon. If you can't give me your answer by then, it's all over." ·

"That's not fair." She protested the placing of a deadline.

"This isn't fair," Trace countered and released her, taking his arm from around her shoulders and rolling to his feet.

Pilar was too stunned by his unexpected desertion so soon after his ultimatum that she couldn't react. He stood for an instant, looking down at her. All expression seemed wiped from his features, yet there was something poignant and lonely about him.

"Think on it, Pilar," he said and moved away to leave her sitting alone on the barge.

Chapter Twelve

*H*er fingers curled tightly around the railing as she felt the glare of the afternoon sun striking her face. Pilar felt trapped by the loud drone of the engines, steadily pushing them upstream. She wanted them to slow down or stop, anything to postpone their arrival in Natchez and give her more time. Her nerves screamed with the tension of knowing that she had a little over an hour at best.

Trace emerged from the pilothouse, his glance running over her before he approached. Pilar turned her face into the breeze, making a show of shaking aside black strands of hair from her cheek. Her body was rigid with the strain of these last hours.

"Want a cold drink? I'm going below to get something for Dan and me." In all their conversation since last night, Trace had skirted the issue between them.

"No." Her answer was stiff and to the point, mostly because she couldn't keep up the casual pretense anymore. The situation was too serious for idle chatter.

After hesitating an instant longer, Trace headed for the ladder, and she listened to the easy run of his footsteps as he descended it. She blinked at the tears that smarted in her eyes, aware that she was feeling sorry for herself because she didn't know what to do.

When Dan Morgan suddenly stepped out of the pilothouse, she avoided looking at him so he wouldn't see the distress in her expression. But he paid no attention to her, hurrying by to the forward railing.

"Hey, Trace!" There was an urgency in his shout. "We've got trouble! Three runaway barges are coming downstream! It just came over the radio!"

Hard on the heels of his call of alarm came the clanging noise of Trace racing up the ladder. Pilar turned from the railing, not fully understanding what kind of trouble this represented but silently hoping that it would bring about some kind of delay. Morgan hovered by the steps until Trace appeared. Together they walked swiftly toward the pilothouse while Morgan gave him the details of the situation.

"A towboat lost power upstream and hit the highway bridge at Natchez. He was pushing all empty oil barges. Three of them broke loose," Morgan explained as they went inside and Pilar followed to listen. There was a tenseness in Morgan's glance when he paused. "Trace, one of those barges has a fire in the hold."

Swearing under his breath, Trace moved to look at the river charts. "When did it happen?"

"Ten, fifteen minutes at the most."

"Damn," Trace muttered, pausing only a second in his study of the charts. "Alert the crew. Have them start looking for the smoke. In this current, and empty besides, those barges will be on top of us before we know it. We're going to have to get out of the channel." He glanced out the window, checking their present position.

"You know this river better than I do," Morgan conceded after he'd warned the crew of the impending trouble via the loudspeaker intercom aboard. "You just tell me where you want her to go and I'll take her there."

"Start turning starboard," Trace advised and stepped to the door. "With the river this high, we should be able to hug that section of bank coming up and still have water under us."

"And if you're wrong?" Pilar murmured.

He threw her a short glance. "Then we're in a lot more trouble."

Everything seemed to be happening on the other side of the boat, so Pilar shifted to the starboard deck. All the crew, everyone, seemed to be holding their breath as the towboat and its barges eased toward the bank under Trace's directions. The rolling water was the color of pale milk chocolate, thick and churning next to the bank. They drew close enough for Pilar to make out the striated bark on the trees growing at the river's edge.

"Power down and hold her in place against the current," Trace ordered, and Pilar felt the changing pitch of the engines as Morgan signaled the change in speed to the engine room.

A voice squawked over the walkie-talkie. "I can see the smoke." It was Tucker Smith, from his position at the bow of one of the lead barges.

Her gaze flashed to the front where gray-black smoke was billowing against the flat horizon. But the barges themselves were not in sight, hidden by the far bend in the river.

"Anything yet?" Trace snapped the question at Morgan.

"Won't be able to get a fix on them until they come around that point," he answered, watching the radar screen intently.

"Come on, Pilar." The rough grip of his hand clasped her high on the arm and aimed her toward the ladder. "I want you on the lower deck." He followed her down, as if to insure that she went.

"Here they come." One of the deckhands passed Trace a pair of binoculars, which he trained on dark shapes belching black smoke.

From the top deck Morgan shouted, "Trace!"

"I see them!" He raised his voice to answer,

then made a sweep of the intervening stretch of river with his glasses.

The tension in the air was almost electrical. Pilar's skin seemed to tingle with it as she watched the plume of dark smoke. Everyone seemed poised and motionless, straining to see.

"The current's going to swing them right into us."

"Jeezus! If that fire sets off this sulfur, this whole thing will explode. There won't be anything left of us to find."

The predictions followed one on top of the other, shocking Pilar into an awareness of the full extent of their danger. She looked at Trace, her mouth open with nothing coming out.

"Tie off those barges to the trees!" He was rifling out orders while everyone else was standing around in a numbed trance. "And get ready to cut the boat loose from them. Move!" The crew scattered, scrambling onto the barges, half of them jumping onto the bank to catch the lines thrown by the others. "Evers!" He motioned impatiently for the cook to join them.

"If you've got in mind what I think—" the cook began.

"If I'm going to lose it all, I'm not going to stay here like a sitting duck and wait for it. With those barges tied up front, there was no way we could have outmaneuvered those runaways in the channel. At least now we've got a chance."

"Yeah, but—"

"Don't worry. God takes care of food and losers." It was only Trace's surface attention the cook had; all the rest was trained on the activity of the crew and the distant runaway barges. It gave his remarks an offhand quality. The same impersonal touch was present when he took Pilar by the arm and pushed her into Evers' keeping. "Take Pilar and get her out of here. And don't stay on the barges. Get her up on the levee."

It took her a second to realize that Trace was putting her off the boat. "No! I don't—"

Trace angrily cut across her words. "I don't have time to argue with you!" His glance slashed to the cook as he ordered curtly, "Get her off."

Her arms were pinioned by the cook's hands, preventing her from going after Trace when he strode away to another section of the deck to hurry up the crew. Pilar resisted Evers' attempt to draw her toward the barges.

"I'm staying here," she insisted.

"You'd just be in the way, ma'am," he said through his cigar. "And they're gonna have their hands full just doin' their jobs."

"But if you stayed—"

"Hell, I'm a cook. I ain't no hero. They can risk their damn fool necks if they want, but not me." He forcibly guided her toward the access steps to the barges.

Reluctantly Pilar allowed herself to be driven along while she kept looking back at Trace, but he seemed to have put her from his mind already. At the steps Evers paused next to the large "No Smoking" sign and removed the cigar from his mouth.

He speared it over the side into the water, muttering, "Damn waste." Then he was leading Pilar onto the barges to the starboard side where the barges were being moored to the trees on the bank. Evers made the leap from the barge to the eroded edge of the bank and turned to urge her. "Come on!"

Pilar hesitated, then made the jump across the fast-running water. The bank started to crumble under her feet, but the cook had her by the hands and pulled her onto solid footing. The bowline was the last to be secured, and Pilar turned to watch the forward deckhand sprinting across the barges to the stern. She wanted to stay there and watch what they were going to do, but Evers was tugging at her to follow him.

There was a last glimpse of Trace standing on the top deck by the pilothouse. He seemed to be looking at her, but Pilar couldn't be sure as she was pulled after Evers. The cook broke a path through the scrubby undergrowth along the tree-lined riverbank to the grassy slope of the high levee. Its steep angle forced them to slow their pace to climb to the top, slipping and grabbing at the long grass stems to pull them up.

When they reached the top, they startled half a dozen cows, peacefully grazing on the opposite slope. Slightly out of breath from the climb, Pilar turned to look back at the river.

Separated from the barges, the towboat had reversed clear of them. It made a pivoting swing and headed upstream, angling for the channel. Full power was given to the engines. Without the weight of the barges to slow it down, the towboat seemed to race across the water.

"Look at that baby move out," Evers murmured.

"What are they going to do?" Apprehension shivered through her as she glanced from the towboat to the smoking barges, steadily approaching.

"They're gonna try to get a line on them runaways and push them out of the channel and run 'em aground," he explained, then half muttered to himself, "It's a shame. That boat's so new, it hasn't even got its first paint scratch."

His explanation sounded so matter-of-fact, yet his aside hinted that it wasn't going to be that simple. Her tension grew.

"Is it dangerous?"

"I hope to shout." Evers half laughed the response. "Those barges are running wild in that current. They got a head of steam built up that can sink anything that gets in their way. And the way that current's tossin' them and spinnin' them about, there's no tellin' which way they're goin' next. Those barges could turn that towboat over like it was a paper cup."

"My God," she breathed, her blood suddenly running cold.

"That's not saying it can't be done," he added quickly, as if realizing he had alarmed her.

"But why . . . why is he doing it?" Fear for him prompted her to make the half-angry demand.

"Well, I guess he figures somebody has to, and he's on the scene." The cook shrugged. "His choices weren't all that great. Either way he stood to lose something—the new towboat and the sulfur barges in a big boom if those runaways hit it . . . or badly damaging the towboat if he tried to corral those barges. I don't think Trace figures on it going to the bottom."

The height of the flat-topped levee gave her a panoramic view of the action on the river. Her gaze was riveted to the shiny white towboat, racing on an intercepting course toward the trio of barges tumbling along in the current, the black smoke rolling from one of them, half obscuring the rest. The strain of waiting had her muscles knotted in tight coils as the two came closer and closer. Confusion burst through her when she suddenly noticed that the towboat was passing the barges.

"Aren't they going to try to stop them?" Even as she asked the question, Pilar was frantically hoping that Trace had changed his mind.

"You don't get in front of a charging bull. You circle around behind and grab its tail," Evers advised her.

For a long span of minutes she lost sight of

the towboat in the dense smoke pouring from the hold of the outside barge. Then it emerged and appeared to take aim on the near barge. All the while the current was sweeping them downstream toward the moored sulfur barges.

"He's staying clear of the one that's on fire, and pickin' the one farthest away from it." He explained the reasons behind the choice while he strained to see every maneuver. "Look!" Evers excitedly grabbed her arm. "He's steadying them!"

It took a second for Pilar to realize what he meant. Then she noticed that the loose barges were no longer directionless. They were steadily being pushed crosscurrent. They would miss the sulfur barges.

"Look! They're gettin' a line on it now." He drew her attention to the figure of a man on the runaway barge, working to secure a line on the port side.

At this point the vessels were nearly level with their position on the levee. It was all happening right in front of her. One of the crew was standing on the starboard side, ready to throw a line to the deckhand on the barge.

Suddenly the turbulent, eddying current caught the partially secured barges and swung them around, slamming the near barge broadside into the towboat. Her heart went into her throat as Pilar watched the boat shudder from the violent force of the hit.

"Jeezus, he went over the side," the cook breathed out. When Pilar looked, there was no one standing on the starboard point of the bow. Two men were racing to the place where he'd been. Suddenly there was a head bobbing to the surface in the brown water. "He kept a hold of the line." Relief sighed through his voice as the two men on deck began to drag the third in.

"Who is it? Can you tell?" Anxiety caught her in its grip.

"It's Tucker, I think." Evers made a cautious identification of the dripping man being hauled onto the deck.

The whirling river kept turning them, screening the towboat from her sight behind the thick smoke. Pilar was half sick with fear. Trace was on that tug. If she lost him. . . . A moan came from her throat. With a clarity she wished she had possessed an hour ago, she realized how deeply she loved him. Her teeth came shut on the rising cry of protest that it had taken her so long to see it.

Beside her Evers was anxiously patting his shirt pockets. "Damn, but I wish I had a cigar. What a time to not have any."

Half blinded by tears, she could barely make out the white-painted towboat. After that broadside smash, it was back under power. It made another swing at the barge to secure the starboard line as the swollen river swiftly carried it downstream. The wind blew the hot, choking smoke toward the levee.

"With the heat from that fire, it must be like a furnace down there," Evers declared with a small shake of his head. "I've seen oil fires burn so hot, they just curl a man's hairs—like singeing pinfeathers off a chicken."

It was a detail that merely added to her mounting concern for Trace's safety—and the safety of everyone on board. Her whole system seemed to be working overtime—her heart, her lungs, her nerves, her senses. All were functioning at top speed. Only the time was going slow.

"It looks like they got it secured," the cook observed cautiously. His angle of sight was not the best. "They seem to have it under control, leastwise."

It had all been unfolding in front of her for so long that Pilar had forgotten the twisting turn the Mississippi made a half mile downstream. As the distance increased, it gradually dawned on her that she was going to lose sight of them.

"Hey! Where are you goin'?" Evers reached out to check her when she started to brush past him to hurry along the levee after the disappearing vessels.

"We aren't going to be able to see what's happening when they go around that bend," she explained quickly, unconsciously pulling against his restraining grip.

"Do you have any idea how far that is or how long it would take you to cover it afoot?" he challenged with tolerance. "By the time you got there, they'd probably be another mile downstream."

"But—" She wanted to argue against his claim, but she knew it was hopeless to think she could run fast enough to catch up with them.

"Besides—" Evers put the clincher on his argument. "They'll likely drive the barges aground on the opposite bank, well clear of the channel. The river's so wide at that point, you wouldn't be able to see anything anyway." There was an understanding look in his eyes. "We're better off waitin' here till they come back."

Reluctantly Pilar was forced to agree with his opinion. He had a better grasp of the situation than she did, and more knowledge about what was likely to happen. She was reacting strictly on an emotional level.

But the waiting was agony. She kept watching the smoke in the sky, tracking their probable location on the river by it. It kept getting farther and farther away. It seemed an agony of time before it appeared stationary. The fast chopping noise of a helicopter's rotary blades gradually grew louder. Pilar finally spotted it, flying above the river. A few minutes later fireboats rounded the far bend.

"Help's on its way." Evers acknowledged their imminent arrival on the scene. "They'll be heading back soon. We might as well make our way down to the barges and wait for 'em there."

She followed behind the cook as he edged his way down the steep slope of the levee to the trees and underbrush on the bank. He crashed his way through it, then waited for her.

"Can you make it?"

The high water had undermined the bank, making the footing less solid for the return jump, but Pilar nodded. She took a short, running start and landed hard on her feet atop the barge. The cook joined her right afterward.

Shielding her eyes from the glare of the sun off the water, she anxiously watched for the towboat to come around the river bend. It seemed the longest wait she had ever made in her life. She was about to decide something was wrong when she finally saw it.

"There it is!" she choked on a sob of relief as she eagerly pointed it out to the cook.

The *Santee Lady* showed the scars of her battle to bring the runaway barges under control. Her hull was scraped and scratched, and her white paint was grimy with the soot and smoke from the fire. In places it even appeared scorched by the fierce heat.

An exhausted crew lounged on her decks, rousing themselves with an effort when the battered towboat approached the moored barges. Pilar waited impatiently while it was maneuvered into position, searching the decks for a glimpse of Trace to verify to her own satisfaction that he was unharmed.

"Hey, Evers! You missed all the fun!" The deckhand Billy Bob Davis hopped onto the barge to tie off the port line.

"Yeah, well, I had a grandstand seat," the cook countered the jibing taunt. "Who went in the drink?"

"Tucker."

"Thought so." Evers kept a hand on Pilar's arm, making her wait until the towboat made its swing to the starboard to make itself fast to the barges.

The minute they scrambled onto the boat's deck, they were practically enveloped by the crew, eager to recount their heroics. Pilar kept looking for Trace, finally catching sight of him as he made his way down the ladder to her level.

"I thought I was a goner," Tucker was saying. "I could feel that undertow pulling me down. And, man, I had a grip on that rope—"

"Yeah, he did," Joe Allen interrupted with a laugh. "Even after we got him back aboard, he didn't wanna let go of it."

"It was like an inferno close to that fire . . ."

Pilar ceased to listen as Trace approached the group. She was content just to look at him, making sure he had all his fingers and toes. Like the rest of the crew, he was smoke-grimed. On his shirt were damp patches and the drying stains of perspiration from the excessive heat. The hairs on his arms were singed, but he appeared otherwise unharmed.

A broad, reckless smile was on his face, and his gray eyes were aglitter with the aftermath of adventure. In a way he had enjoyed it, she realized. He could have gotten himself killed, but he had enjoyed it, while she had been crazy with worry.

A lump came to her throat. It was impossible to be angry with him. It was too crazy, and she was too happy just knowing he was all right. Tears welled in her eyes, turning them black and brilliant. His smiling glance finally strayed to her. There was nothing in his expression to suggest that it had ever occurred to him that she had been worried for his safety. It changed to a puzzled little half-smile when he noticed the tears in her eyes.

"Hey. What's this?" He bent his head slightly to peer at her, teasing and curious.

"You crazy fool," she declared in a voice thickened with emotion.

Some inner force impelled her into his arms. She hugged him tightly and buried her face in his shirt, mindless of its rank smell of smoke and sweat. Just to hear the sound of his heartbeat and to feel the solid strength of his body was a kind of bliss.

Her sudden action had taken him by surprise. It was a beat later before his arms circled to hold her and he bent his head, still vaguely startled by her emotional reaction. She felt the warmth of his breath stirring her hair and closed her eyes at the sweetness of the sensation. It squeezed a tear from her lashes and sent it trickling down her cheek.

"You're going to get all dirty," he advised her huskily. As the roughness of his hand cupped her cheek, he felt the wetness of that tear and tilted her head back so that he could examine her face. "Hey, what's wrong?"

For a second all she could do was look at

him, knowing at last how much he meant to her. "I'd have died if I lost you, Trace." It was a choked whisper, vibrant with feeling.

His gray eyes suddenly darkened, alive and searching with an intense longing in them that tore at her heart. She finally came to appreciate some of the torment he'd endured over her after the agonizing hours she'd spent that afternoon.

"You don't have to wait until we get to Natchez, Trace," she told him softly. "I love you and that's all that matters."

The touch of his lips was wonderfully tentative. For a minute his arms held her as if he'd been given something precious beyond worth and he was afraid of breaking it. But she kissed him back with fierce ardor to show him that the love she felt for him was strong enough to take anything. His mouth hardened in its possession of hers as his molding hands shaped her to his length.

Slowly and discreetly the crew wandered away from them and pretended they didn't notice a thing. But here and there a small pleased smile showed at the picture the captain and his lady made together.

FREE

THE DAILEY NEWSLETTER

Would you like to know more
about Janet Dailey and her newest novels?
The Janet Dailey Newsletter is filled
with information about Janet's life, her
travels and appearances with her
husband Bill, and advance information on
her upcoming books—plus comments
from Janet's readers, and a personal letter
from Janet in each issue. The Janet
Dailey Newsletter will be sent to you <u>free</u>.
Just fill out and mail the coupon
below. If you're already a subscriber,
send in the coupon for a friend!

POCKET BOOKS

The Janet Dailey Newsletter
Pocket Books
Dept. JDN
1230 Avenue of the Americas
New York, N.Y. 10020

Please send me Janet Dailey's Newsletter.

NAME_____

ADDRESS_____

CITY_____STATE_____ZIP_____

651